Two Novels

Seventeen

J

Two Novels

Seventeen

J

Kenzaburo Oe

Introduction by Masao Miyoshi

Translated from the Japanese by Luk Van Haute

Foxrock Books
New York

Introduction Copyright © 1996 by Masao Miyoshi

First published in 1991 by: North Star Line
This edition published in 2002 by: Foxrock Books

Foxrock, Inc.
61 Fourth Avenue
New York, NY 10003

Cover design by Steve Brower
Cover art by Jeremiah Nathan

ISBN #1-56201-091-3

Manufactured in the United States of America

Introduction

by Masao Miyoshi

The sixties began early in Japan. While the Japanese economy expanded by leaps and bounds after the War, much of it was thanks to U.S. cold war patronage, the strain of the contradictions between rising material ease and widening social fragmentation—economic pride and political shame—had been ever acute since Japan began to recover from a near-zero productivity at the time of its defeat in 1945. The tension nearly exploded toward the end of the 1950s.

In early 1960, Premier Nobusuke Kishi, formerly a Class-A defendant in the Tokyo War Crime Tribunal, signed a new Mutual Security Treaty with the United States and sought its ratification in the Diet. Fierce opposition broke out from a loose coalition of unionists, Communists, students and scholars, women, and urban voters who feared the further surrender of Japan to the United States. These groups also feared the erosion of civil rights finally granted them after the brutality of World War II, itself a disaster resulting from a century of imperial militarism. Kishi resorted to parliamentary manipulations and, by physically removing the Lower House opposition members from the Diet building, rammed through the ratification in June.

In the first half of 1960, the country rocked with protests and demonstrations that often mobilized waves of activists numbering hundreds of thousands onto the streets of Tokyo and around the Diet building in particular. In the aftermath of Kishi's strong-armed tactics, the outraged opposition forced the cancellation of President Eisenhower's plan to visit Japan for the celebration of the U.S.-Japan alliance, and ultimately toppled the Kishi cabinet. In the long run, the effect of the 1960 protest was perhaps minimal: Japan was securely chained to U.S. foreign policy, and the domination of the conservative Liberal Democratic Party remained unshaken for over thirty years. Nevertheless, this was the first time in Japan's history that people seriously challenged the power and authority of the government. It was into this political turbulence that Kenzaburo Oe, born in 1935, reached his precocious maturity as a writer.

There was a particular circumstance that occasioned Oe's writing of *Seventeen*. After the Diet was dissolved, the chairman of the Socialist Party was stabbed to death in October 1960, while engaged in a public debate for the upcoming election. Over the summer there had been several political murder attempts (including one by an extreme right-winger on Prime Minister Kishi), and yet this assassination especially shocked the nation because the National Broadcasting Corporation captured the entire event on film. The culprit, seized on camera, was a seventeen-year-old terrorist named Otoya Yamaguchi, determined to fulfill his life's goal by killing a "traitorous" leftist leader. The attack was made even more sensational as the youthful "patriot" hanged himself three weeks later in a juvenile penitentiary. Before his suicide Yamaguchi scribbled on a wall, "Service for my country seven lives over. Long live His Majesty the Emperor."

This violent history did not end there. In December of the same year, a writer named Fukazawa Shichiro wrote a bizarre dream-take about Emperor Hirohito's family, describing their public decapitation in a revolution. Another right-wing youth—he too happened to be seventeen years old—was enraged by what in his eyes amounted to a blasphemy and found his way into the home of Shichiro's publisher. Failing to find the publisher, he plunged a knife into his wife and killed her maid.

Oe published *Seventeen* in January 1961. The story tells of an adolescent modeled after Yamaguchi, who saves himself from self-hatred and depression by joining a right-wing gang. In its sequel, *A Political Youth Dies*, published the following month, Oe represents the juvenile activist's final deliverance through assassination and suicide. He freely mixed the known details of Yamaguchi's life into his portrait in the two novelettes. Details are drawn with oppressive sordidness, especially in *Seventeen*. The right-wing reaction was instantaneous. Oe received threatening letters from ultra-nationalistic gangsters who were infuriated by his insults to the emperor and his depiction of their young hero as a compulsive masturbator. Someone hurled rocks at his study; a dozen right-wing thugs screeched menacing threats in front of his house; and midnight phone calls never stopped. Oe's thoroughly frightened publisher offered apologies to his readers in the March issue of the journal, alienating Oe this time from the readers on the left (which included a woman who swore to attack Oe for his "cowardly acquiescence" with the compromising publisher). The history of these events is detailed in his later "fiction," *Letters to the Memorable Year* (1987), where an account of his youthful self not fully comprehending his own political position rings painfully true:

> I blamed myself that I did not handle *Seventeen* and *A Political Youth Dies* with greater skill. That is, I could have written without provoking the right wing and yet making my message more forthright. I could have done this here, done that there . . . such thoughts kept recurring. My regret always ended in the shame that I had lost all prospects of book publishing in the face of rightist threats, while having to receive letters from the left wing every day that charged me with cowardice—all this because of my careless way of writing. Worse, I even felt that novel writing was itself an irremediable error of my life . . . . I gave up French studies by turning into a novelist and essayist. As a result I couldn't even count myself among my college classmates. It was too late to start all over again as a scholar of French literature . . . .

In the face of threats from the right and contempt from the left, Oe was suicidally depressed for two years between 1961 and 1963. In the highly politicized sixties, the pressure on writers to announce their commitments and affiliations was immense, and the scrutiny and interrogations were ruthless. In 1963 he wrote *Sexual Humans (Seiteki ningen)* a novella with the title as odd in Japanese as to be nearly untranslatable, hence in this volume altered to *J*, the protagonist's name. It expresses the nadir of Oe's anguish and depression in the Dolce Vita mood of decadence and abandon in its first half, and in the rapist sublimation through commuter-train molestation in the second part.

Oe had been enormously prolific. Early in 1958 he had already received the Akutagawa Prize, a prestigious award, while he was still a twenty-three-year-old undergraduate. By the time he wrote *Seventeen* and *A Political Youth Dies* in 1961 at the age of twenty-six, he had published numerous stories, novellas (e.g., *Nip the Buds, and Shoot the Kids*; 1958), and essays. A glamorous, brainy author, he was surrounded by an admiring circle of readers, critics, and scholars who saw in him a promise greater than any in his peers, including Yukio Mishima, who was Oe's senior by ten years. His model-student background was enhanced by the support given by his mentors in literature and academia, many of them associated with the University of Tokyo. In 1960 he married Yukari Itami, the beautiful daughter of Mansaku Itami who introduced film to Japan early in the century and the sister of Juzo, the best-known director in Japan now, who was Oe's high-school friend. He was defiant in challenging the literary conventions and bourgeois codes but was never reckless. He met Mao Zedong and Jean Paul Sartre in his travels abroad around this time. Too academic and too literary to be an unambiguous political activist, Oe was always performing a "solemn tight-rope walk," as he called it with self-irony in his first collection of essays in 1965. This "ambiguity" lasts to this day—even after he named his Nobel acceptance speech in 1994 "Japan the Ambiguous and Myself."

Seventeen is so resolute in its rejection of the right-wing extremism that it unavoidably turns into a hyperbolic caricature of a fanatic adolescent, betraying along the way signs of discomfort about sexuality that are not altogether in the author's control. The obsession with masturbation, for example, is not easy to explain in terms of the young man's psychology alone. At the same time, the casual remarks on the Nazi uniform and the Imperial Way Party discipline serve as a prophetic blueprint for Yukio Mishima's last novels as well as his actual life as it draws closer to his suicide ten years later.

A Political Youth Dies (Seiji Shonen Shisu) has never been reprinted in any language after its first appearance in the *Bungakkai* journal in February 1961. The tale is a sequel to *Seventeen* as is made clear by the subtitle, "Seventeen, Part II." The reason Oe gives for his reluctance to reissue it is the threat of the right wing, which is very much alive even today. His brother-in-law, the film director Juzo Itami, was nearly stabbed to death a few years ago after making a film that ridiculed the gangsters. When Oe received the Nobel Prize and refused the Order of Culture from the emperor, the right-wing threats were revived: a truck with a loud speaker was parked in front of his house, broadcasting menacing messages once again; threats to the safety of Oe and his family were issued; posters calling him a traitor were posted all over Tokyo. Under the circumstances, Oe's cautiousness must be respected and, therefore, *A Political Youth Dies* is not included in this volume.

Gangsters, however, are ordinarily not well-trained as literary critics—although I should add in this case that professional critics who have read the novelette since seem also misguided in reading the tale as "leftist" either in praise or complaint. *A Political Youth Dies* is not an anti-rightist propaganda. It may have started out as an attack on Yamaguchi and his colleagues in right-wing terrorism; after all, it was meant to be the continuation of *Seventeen*. And yet even a casual reading would reveal a fundamental difference between *Seventeen* and this work.

True, the narrator is the same seventeen-year-old emperorist. He pursues the program outlined in *Seventeen* to murder a leftist leader, presumably the Socialist Party Chairman, and rage against those who are disloyal to the emperor. In one section of the story, the remarks published by the actual commentators concerning the Yamaguchi incident are quoted with their real names, identifying the two tales with the event of October 1960. What separates this story from both the external Otoya Yamaguchi and the narrator of *Seventeen* however, is its tone, thought, style, sensitivity, responsiveness, and mental alacrity. Vulnerability, anxiety, imaginative vigor, and intelligence, as well as suspiciousness and hostility, are clearly discernible in both the narrator and the characters as seen through him. The adolescent "I" is still an Imperial Way member, and yet he is aware of the subtle differences among its members and among all around. He is endowed with imagination, sensitivity, and curiosity, even about those who would oppose him.

The narrator visits Hiroshima for the atom-bomb anniversary meeting and encounters activists from the left as well as the right. Before long there is a violent confrontation of the opposing groups, and the "I" assaults the progressive students and citizens with brutal force. In his extreme loyalty to the emperor, he is indifferent to issues like humanism, peace, the nuclear bombs, or even war destructions. And yet his record of the trip to Hiroshima has a number of passages that could have been lifted out of Oe's later *Hiroshima Notes*. The reader is introduced to a writer whose name, Seishiro Nambara, more than faintly resembles the name of Kenzaburo Oe in kanji, his customary trick in fiction. The writer is a fearful, intellectual, gay leftist; the type most despised by the radical right-wingers. The drunken weakling displays unexpected courage, however, quietly declaring his intention to fight back should the thugs choose to attack him. In this confrontation scene, care is taken to make sure that both parties be allowed to talk with each other with little authorial intervention. After the trip to Hiroshima the narrator begins to distrust his party that seems too comfortable with peaceful life. He misses the glory of the fight that he enjoyed at the time of the Security Treaty struggle. During his desperate search for belief and certainty, he has a revelation and sees the vision of the emperor. Bliss is attainable in the ecstasy of action for the absolute.

The scene of the assassination is described in a combination of the second person and the third. Either way, the voice of the adolescent is replaced here by quotations from several TV commentators and journalists. Before the tale reaches this portion, however, the dominant perspective of his dramatic monologue is largely appropriated by the terrorist youth. It is not that the work has abandoned its critical position on imperial absolutism and rightist extremism. Only the distance of contempt that kept the characters of *Seventeen* from the reader vanishes. There is a sort of intense sympathy that refuses to be taken lightly. The loneliness of the young man unmistakably inscribed in the texture and feeling and thoughts that were largely absent in *Seventeen.* Similarly, the freedom and relief that the narrator experiences in solitary jail cell is not that of a murderous fanatic who gloats over his accomplishment, but that of a sensitive youth who has finally escaped the impossible pressure of his mission, having fulfilled the absolute dictate of his revelation. What is conveyed is not the structure of terrorist ideas but the existential authenticity of his craving for belief and certainty, a dangerously contagious crisis and a desperate facing up against it. Finally, the substance of the novelette could be taken to have little to do with the ideologies of the right or the left.

The story can be read as an anti-fascist statement, or the reverse, namely that *A Political Youth Dies* reveals Oe to have a rightist double in himself, and that despite his announced anti-emperorism, he hides the awe of the monarch that was ingrained into him while still a young boy during World War II. However, it might be more insightful to read the story as possessing the energies of belief and disbelief, or political commitment and disengagement, or action and reflection, or even fiction and nonfiction. Oe's postwar embrace of freedom and democracy, for instance, is subtly entangled with a distrust of such humanist celebration. Ambiguity is ineradicable here. But instead of being at ease with ambiguity, Oe seems compelled to question its instability, to work it through to arrive at unambiguity, certitude. Unambiguity of ambiguity, or ambiguity of unambiguity. The process is endless, and in this shifting complexity, Oe's work nearly always grows its roots.

Those who are curious about Oe's discipline in producing *A Political Youth Dies* should read *Runaway Horses, Part Two* of the tetrology *The Sea of Fertility*, which Yukio Mishima wrote ten years later. The tale is also about a young right-wing assassin who too takes his own life after murdering a political potentate for the glory of the emperor. The settings are, of course, quite different, as Mishima was always susceptible to the stylish glamour of a revue-like theatricality. But even here, some imagery resembles Oe's work. As the hero commits harakiri at the end, for instance, he has the vision of a glorious emblazing sun.

As far as I know no one has pointed out Mishima's heavy borrowing, if not outright plagiarism, of the younger writer's earlier work. At the same time, Mishima's identification with the handsome young boy is embarrassingly unguarded and unqualified. His pronouncement of the emperorist program, too, is so transparent that *Runaway Horses* is nearly unreadable—except as part of Mishima's biography. This—Mishima's self-indulgence and Oe's discipline—might be the greatest difference that lies between the two writers.

Oe published *Sexual Humans (Seiteki Ningen)* in May 1963, more than two years after the two political tales. Just as *Seventeen* was subdivided into two parts of *Seventeen* and *A Political Youth Dies*, *Sexual Humans (J* hereafter) is also composed of two parts. According to Oe's scheme as explained in "A Solemn Tight-Rope Walk," "sexual" and "political" are counterpoised to each other though they seem also integral in a complicated way. Thus, a chain of dialectics, or a series of binaries, is his intellectual consistency. And again there is the ecstasy of action for the absolute.

It is fascinating to note that the young *chikan* boy's unfinished poetic masterpiece has the title of "A Solemn Tight-Rope Walk," the title of Oe's actual essay discussing *Seventeen* and *J*. Oe says he himself wanted once to write a collection of poems while he was in his twenties under the title of *A Solemn Tight-Rope Walk*. The adjective, he explains, means that what appeared to the others as an absurd balancing act was for himself a dead-serious performance. Oe knew that he was being watched, and he was frightened. After eight years of fear, brief reliefs, and blinding despair, he still didn't know what he had learned from the balancing act. He does not make clear what he was trying to balance at the time. As for politics, he was clearly on the side of the sovereignty of the individual citizen as against the external absolute authority (*"Kenpo ni tsuite no kojinteki na taiken"*). He was also firmly for the renunciation of war, and he was troubled by the recent retroversion to the prewar ideology among some people.

There is no doubt that in Oe's earlier writing the political and the sexual were intimately connected, but what exactly the relationship was is far from clear. They are in contrast: political as combative versus sexual as assimilative, for example; or the political as rejecting the absolute, while the sexual as accepting the absolute (*"Warera no sei no sekai"*). How this scheme works in the context of *Seventeen*, *A Political Youth Dies*, and *J* (*"Sexual Humans"*), I and II, is not easy to decipher. Is politics represented by the narrator's general hostility in *Seventeen*? Is the absolute being accepted in the two parts of *J*? How? At any rate, what does become clear is that Oe in the 1960s seems to have been carefully distancing himself from both politicality and sexuality no matter how the two were related to each other. In this view, politics is inevitably mastur-batory, as *Seventeen* seems strongly to suggest. But then sexuality, too, unavoidably leads to autoeroticism, even when it victimizes a woman in the act of molestation. There seems to be no exit in either route.

Seventeen

1

TODAY IS MY BIRTHDAY. Seventeen years of age I am today: a Seventeen.* But nobody in my family realizes it's my birthday. Not my father, not my mother or my brother. Or at least they act like they don't. So I keep quiet about it too.

Toward evening, my older sister comes home from the Self-Defense Forces hospital, where she works as a nurse. I'm in the bathroom, lathering myself with soap. "Seventeen years old," she calls out to me. "Doesn't it just make you want to grab yourself?"

My sister is horribly nearsighted, and so ashamed of her glasses she's made up her mind never to get married. That's why she went to work for the SDF. In desperation, she does nothing but read. She's ruining her eyes all the more, but she doesn't care.

*Translator's note: An American word in the Japanese text referring to the American magazine, an important symbol to the young Japanese of that period, just as it was to American adolescents.

SEVENTEEN

What she said to me now was probably stolen from a book. Still, at least one person in the family remembered my birthday. As I scrub myself down, I recover just a little from my lonéliness. I repeat what my sister said. As I think about her words, my sex stands up out of the soap in a sudden erection. I go and lock the bathroom door.

It seems like I'm always having erections. I like erections. I like them because of the sensation of energy boiling up through my body. And I like to look at my sex in the state of erection. I sit down again and cover myself with soap from head to foot. Then I masturbate. My first masturbation since I turned seventeen.

At first I wondered if masturbation wasn't bad for me, but I looked through some sexology books in the bookstore and made the liberating discovery that the only bad thing about masturbation is feeling guilty about it.

I don't like the reddish-black adult sex, looking completely naked with the skin peeled back, and I don't like kids' sex, which looks like some kind of unripe plant. The sex I like is my own, when it's ready for masturbation. My very own sex. I can pull back the foreskin if I want to, but when I have an erection, it covers the rose-colored head like a soft sweater. I can use it to warm the stuff under the skin and melt it into a lubricating oil.

During health class, the school doctor told us how to get rid of that stuff, but everybody laughed. That's because we all masturbate, so there's never any stuff to get rid of. I've gotten to be quite a "hand" at masturbation. I've even discovered how to grab the tip of my foreskin as I come, like I'm squeezing the neck of a bag, and catch the semen in it. As a further advance, I've also made a side door in the pocket of a pair of pants. When I wear those, I can masturbate even in class.

As I masturbate now, I recall a story I saw in the color feature of a women's magazine, the confessions of a husband who gave his wife peritonitis by ramming his penis through the wall of her vagina on their wedding night. My erect sex is wrapped in its soft white foreskin, cloaked in a blue haze. It strains upward with the powerful beauty of a rocket. As I caress it, I realize for the very first time that the muscles of my arms are beginning to grow.

For a moment I stare in amazement at my muscles. They're like new rubber straps. My muscles. I grab my own muscular flesh, like my sister said. Joy wells up inside me. I smile. I'm a Seventeen, with no love for anybody but myself. My triceps, my biceps, my thigh muscles, they're all still young and immature, but with training they'll grow unfettered into thick sinewy muscle.

I think about asking my father to buy me an expander or a barbell set for my birthday. The old man is a tightwad, and he's not about to spend money on things like training equipment, but the warm steam and the soft soap bubbles have put me into the kind of rapture where it seems like I could talk him into it. By next summer my body will be solid, developed everywhere it ought to be. It'll catch the eyes of the girls at the beach, and plant fervent roots of respect in the hearts of the boys in my class. The salt taste of the sea breeze, the hot sand, the itching powder dusted over sunburned skin, the smell of me and my friends, and amid the cries of the naked crowd of swimmers, an abyss of blissful dizziness into which I suddenly plunge, in silence and solitude. I cry out and close my eyes. The hard hot sex in my grip stiffens for an instant, and in that instant I feel the sperm that erupts from inside me flowing out to fill my hand. All the while, I know that the lucky crowd of naked bathers is peacefully swimming, sunken into silence in the clear summer afternoon sea within me.

Then the chill of an autumn afternoon comes to call on the sea inside my body. I shiver and open my eyes. The bathroom floor is spattered with semen from one end to the other. Already it's nothing but a cold, hypocritical, murky white fluid. I don't feel like it's mine. I run hot water everywhere to wash it away, but the spongy last lumps get stuck between the boards and won't wash out for love or money. If my sister sits down on there, she might get pregnant. That's incest, and my sister will probably turn into a filthy lunatic.

I keep on running hot water, but while I'm at it, I get cold and feel like I'm about to start shivering. I get into the tub but I get out almost as soon as I get in, making a lot of noise as I splash around. If I'm in the bath too long, my mother's sure to get suspicious. Then she gets sarcastic. "Until last year this kid was like a bird in the bath. What's this sudden interest in the tub, I'd like to know."

Kenzaburo Oe

I'm fuming as I unlock the door, making sure I don't
make a sound. When I come out of the bathroom the happiness that came boiling up at the moment of orgasm, like
something was thronging together from inside and outside
my body at the same time, the friendship I felt for people I
didn't know from Adam, the feeling of life lived in common,
all the dregs of those feelings stay trapped in the steam,
which has a slight tang of semen.

A large mirror is hanging against the wall of the little
dressing room. I see my lonely self standing there naked and
dejected in the yellow light. I'm a dejected Seventeen if there
ever was one. My sex has shriveled back into my crotch
where the hair, if you can even call it that, grows only in bare
wisps. My foreskin has shrunk up to look like a wrinkled
blue-black chrysalis. It hangs down wet and heavy, from
sucking up water on the one hand and semen on the other.
Only my balls are relaxed by the hot water, and they look
like they want to hang down to my knees. It is an unappealing sight. What's more, with the light behind me now, the
body in the mirror is nothing but skin and bone, and anything but muscle. In the bathroom the lighting was better,
that's all. The realization takes the heart right out of me.

I'm utterly depressed as I put on my shirt. My face
pops out of the collar, staring at me. I come up to the mirror
and take a close look at my face. It's a disgusting face. It's not
that it's ugly or swarthy, it is simply a disgusting face. For
starters, the skin is too thick. It's white and thick like the
skin of a pig. I like a face with thin, tanned skin stretched

tight over good clean cheekbones, like a runner's face, but under my skin there's a mass of flesh and fat. It gives the impression that the one fat part of me is my face.

Then there's my narrow forehead. With my coarse hair pressing in on it, it looks even smaller than it is. My cheeks are swollen, but my lips are small and red, and look like a girl's. My eyebrows are heavy and short, growing without life, and have no clear shape, and my eyes are narrow and tend to roll back in my head, showing too much white around the bottoms, which gives me a nasty look.

And my ears. My ears are those fleshy "lucky Buddha ears" that stick straight out from the sides of my head.

My face seems to be ashamed of its flabby, girlish look. Every time I have my picture taken I end up feeling completely beaten. Especially when they take the class picture of everybody in my grade at school; the photo comes out so depressing I want to die. The photographer always makes a second print with my face retouched to look smooth and round as an egg.

I glare at my face in the mirror, wanting to groan. I've turned bluish-black. That's the facial color of a chronic masturbator. At school and in town maybe I'm actually a walking advertisement for the fact that I'm always masturbating. Maybe other people know about my masturbation habit as soon as they see me. Maybe they can see through me, every time they see my big ugly nose: Look! He's one who does you-know-what. Maybe they gossip about it.

I can't help feeling the same way I did when I thought

masturbation was bad for me. Come to think of it, things haven't improved a bit since then. By *things* I mean that I'd be so ashamed if people knew about my masturbating that I'd want to die. Ah, that! people probably say. That guy's a full-time masturbator. Look at the color of his face. Look at those cloudy eyes. They probably look at me and spit, like they're seeing something disgusting. I'd like to kill them. I'd like to machine-gun them to death, every last one of them. I say it out loud. "I want to kill them. With a machine gun, every last one of them. I want to kill them all. If only I had a machine gun!"

My voice is low, and the breath which fails to become a voice steams up the mirror. Instantly I thrust my angry face out of sight behind the haze of dirty fog. What a liberating feeling of freedom it would be, I think spitefully, if my face could disappear this same way from the eyes of all the others who look at me and laugh. But that kind of miracle won't happen. I'm a chronic masturbator who'll always be naked to the eyes of others. A Seventeen who's always doing you-know-what.

I realize this is the first time in my life I've felt so bad on my birthday. And for the rest of my life, all my birthdays will probably be just as bad, if not worse. There's no doubt in my mind that this is a true premonition.

If only I hadn't jerked off. I repent. I have a headache. In despair, as I pull on the rest of my clothes, I start to croon "Oh, Carol."

You hurt me, and you made me cry, but if you leave me,

I will surely die.
Oh, oh, Carol! You treat me cruel!

~

During supper, nobody says anything suitable for my birthday. My sister refuses to repeat even as much as what she
came into the bathroom to say to me. In the end, I realize
that there just isn't anything you can say about my seventeenth birthday. My family never had the habit of talking
while we eat. My old man is the headmaster of a private
high school, and hates talking at mealtime. He thinks it's an
unforgivably vulgar habit for families to talk while they eat.

I seem to be worn out after masturbating, and my head
is throbbing. I feel like I'm mud-spattered with the nastiness
of being a Seventeen, so I don't want to say I'm unhappy
that they can finish their dinner in silence. I myself have
come to think that my birthday should be treated with the
same cold indifference as every other day of my life.

But after dinner I'm dawdling over my tea while I eat
some Korean pickles. I'm not thinking about my birthday
or about the expander, but it might just be that, after all,
somewhere in my heart, there's still some part of me left that
wants to make an issue out of my birthday.

I'm rereading the evening paper and watching television out of the corner of my eye while I drink my tea and
munch on the Korean pickles. I remember a big Korean boy
in my class was always bullying me during my junior high

school days, which I spent in the country. He said it was because I was a dwarf.

The television news shows the Crown Prince and the Crown Princess Michiko delivering a message about their trip overseas. The cunning eyes of the Crown Prince look into the distance as he says something like, "We intend to do our best to be able to live up to the expectations of all the people of Japan."

Michiko is at his side, smiling a slightly forced smile and staring in the direction of us, the people of Japan. I mutter under my breath.

"The tax-stealing parasite has a lot of nerve, the way he talks. I don't expect one damned thing from him."

My sister has been stretched out beside the television reading a paperback, but when I say that she jumps up like an avenging angel and snaps at me.

"Who are you calling parasite?" she says. "You're the one who's got nerve."

That stops me for a minute. I feel like I must've said something wrong. But my old man sits there puffing a cigarette, with his back turned like he could care less, and my older brother, who works for a television station, is oblivious to everything except the model airplane he's putting together. My mother is working in the kitchen, but she has her head screwed around so she can see the television. She's watching it with a fascination that borders on idiocy. Nobody has the least interest in the argument between me and my sister. I'm getting more and more fed up. I'm up on my feet, giving my sister back as good as I'm getting.

"The parasites are the Royal Couple. We don't want anything from those bastards. And if we're going to talk about parasites, I could name a few more. The Self-Defense Forces are at the top of the list. Or didn't you know that? Maybe you're too close to the lighthouse to see the light?"

"Let's leave aside Their Majesties the Crown Prince and Princess," my sister whispers in an ice-cold voice, with her narrow eyes strangely set behind her glasses. "Why are the Self-Defense Forces parasites? If there wasn't any SDF, and if the American army wasn't in Japan, what would Japan do for security? And what about the second and third sons from the farming villages who work for the SDF? If there wasn't any SDF, where could they find work?"

I'm stuck. I go to the most progressive high school in Tokyo. We even have demonstrations. When one of my class friends starts badmouthing the SDF I come to their defense, thinking about my sister working as a nurse in an SDF hospital, but still I think I want to be in the left wing. And when it comes to feelings I fit right in with the Left. I've been in marches, and once I got myself called in by the social studies teacher, who's advisor to the school paper, because I wrote a letter to the editor saying high school students ought to participate in the movement against the American bases. But now I have to say something to knock down my sister's argument, and I'm stuck.

"That's the official explanation. It's the party line those Liberal-Democrat bastards use whenever they want to screw the people," I sneer at her, bluffing all the way. "It's what simple-minded people say. That's what makes them such easy prey for those parasites."

"So okay. I'm simple-minded. Why don't you answer my simple question with that complicated mind of yours? Suppose all the foreign forces get out of Japan, and we do away with the Self-Defense Forces. Since that makes Japan a military vacuum do you think, to give one hypothetical example, we're going to be able to turn our relationship with South Korea to Japan's advantage? Japanese fishing boats are already being held around the Syngman Rhee Line. And if some country lands even a handful of troops on Japanese soil, what can we do if we don't have a military of our own?"

"Can't we appeal to the UN? And except for South Korea, you're just trying to stir up trouble when you talk about a handful of troops from some country. No country on earth is going to land an army in Japan. You're just inventing imaginary enemies."

"The UN isn't almighty, you know. And I'm not talking about an invasion from Mars. When some army from this world invades you, that country has its own voice in the UN too. And the UN won't necessarily think about the welfare of Japan. Anyway, just look at the Korean War, or the wars all over Africa. By the time the UN gets there, the war's already on. If there's fighting on Japanese soil for even three days, an awful lot of Japanese are going to die. A UN army isn't going to mean anything to those dead Japanese.

You can say what you like about Japan, but whether some country has Japan for a base or not makes a big difference in the Far East. If America goes home, don't you think the left-wingers are going to want to invite in Soviet military bases so they can sleep a little easier? I have chances to meet American soldiers from the bases, you know, more than you do. So I can say it's not good to have foreign soldiers in Japan. It'd be better to build up the SDF. That way we can also save the second and third farming village sons from unemployment."

I feel like I'm getting beaten on one thing after another, and I don't like it. I don't want to lose. Besides, my position is supposed to be right. When I talk with friends at school, ideas like my sister's get thrown out and beaten into the ground. Nobody takes them seriously for even a second. So I tell myself I have to win now. Shit, I think to spur myself on. The wisdom of woman, I guess. I've never really thought about whether the rearmament is correct.

"Aren't those second and third farmer sons unemployed because of the rotten politics of the Conservative cabinet?" I say. "The unemployed are the result of bad politics, and aren't they just being used again for the sake of more bad politics?"

I'm hot now, but my sister isn't ruffled at all.

"Then what about the postwar recovery and the growth of the economy? That was achieved under the Conservative government that's supposed to be so bad. The Conservative government lets Japan prosper. That's the truth, isn't it?

Isn't that why most Japanese support the Conservative party?"

"Japan's prosperity is shit, and the Japanese who vote for the Conservative party are shit. It's all disgusting," I shout. Tears are running down my face. I feel like an ignorant fool, and I don't know what to do about it.

"That kind of Japan ought to be wiped off the face of the earth, and that kind of Japanese can all go to hell."

My sister hesitates. Then, with cold eyes, like a cat playing with a mouse it's knocked flat, she looks at my face. My tears probably make me look terrible. She looks down, pretending to read the newspaper.

"If that's what you think," she says, "at least you're consistent. But if you ask me, the left-wingers seem to be talking out of both sides of their mouths at the same time. They talk like they're the protectors of democracy, but they don't respect parliamentary government. They blame everything on the tyranny of the majority. They're against rearmament. They call it a violation of the Constitution, but they don't lift a finger to find jobs for members of the SDF. They aren't honest, they only want to be 'anti.' They drink the sweet juice the mixer of Conservative government makes, but then they blame the government for the bitter. It'd be a good thing to let the progressives take power for once in the next election. Let them chase the Americans off the bases, let them destroy the SDF, and then let's see if taxes go down and we get rid of unemployment. Let's see if the economic growth rate soars. It's not like I enjoy being despised as an SDF nurse, you know. To tell the truth, I wouldn't mind being a progressive worker with a clean conscience . . ."

My tears ought to be proof enough that a dirty sense of shame is stuffed inside me like lead from my head to my asshole. My old man and brother, who're ignoring our argument with utter indifference, also give me the feeling of being pushed into a gulf of explosive rage and misery. His son is in tears, and the old man just sits there bathing in complacency, with the newspaper spread in front of him. He thinks that's how you show American-style liberalism.

Even at the private high school where he works, my old man's proud of the fact that he doesn't make the students do anything and never gets involved in their problems, all in the name of American-style liberal education. But I heard from one guy who transferred from my father's school that the old man is hated and despised by his students. You can't count on him to act like a teacher, they think. One time the papers made a stink about it, when about twenty students at his school were supposed to get guidance for some kind of sex trouble, but the old man was unflappable. He said it was his personal belief as a liberal that it isn't permissible to restrict students' behavior after school hours. That's an irresponsible philosophy. Students my age are unstable and rebellious, but what we want most is a teacher who thinks about our problems and gives us a firm shoulder to lean on.

As for me, I sometimes wish he would get involved in my problems, even if he overdid it. At times like this, I don't know whether he's supposed to be American or liberal, but he is more like a stranger than a father.

My father doesn't have any real schooling. He educated himself, struggling along in a lot of different jobs. After he got his license he made it to his present position. So now he does his dead-level best not to get involved with other people, trying to hold on to the position he's got. He's afraid of trouble from other people, of getting embroiled with others and falling back into the pits of society. Even in front of his own son he never takes off the armor of that instinct for self-protection. He doesn't show any emotion, like he doesn't want to show himself naked and lose his dignity. All he ever does is give out cold-blooded, irresponsible criticism. Even now, my old man is probably trying to take the most typical attitude of American-style liberalism . . .

~

My sister is puffed up with victory and goes on muttering comments. I want to go and crawl into the shed that's my little hideout so I won't have to hear them. That's absolutely the only thing I'm thinking about when I stand up. My heart is a swirl of angry humiliation and shame, and there's no room in me to think about anything else.

I stand and take one step forward, and kick the tea table. There is a crash and the cups go flying and cold tea runs out, yellow like piss. For one instant, I hold my breath and look at my father. He doesn't scream at me. Instead, he puts a cool, derisive smile on his lips. He never takes his eyes off the paper.

"Another rampage by the Student Coalition," my sister says mockingly.

I explode. With a scream I give my sister a terrific kick to the forehead. She falls over on her back with her hands still reaching for the table. I see blood where her eyelid was cut by the shattered lens of her glasses. Her grotesque face turns gruesomely pale. Blood trickles from her eyelid, which swells tight over her eye, down to the remarkable elevation of her cheekbone. My mother comes charging out of the kitchen to take care of her.

I'm shocked by what I've done. I stand rooted to the floor, shaking. When I see that my toes are covered with my sister's blood, burning pain and a crawling itch come climbing up my leg. My father slowly lowers his paper to his knees and looks up at me. I wait to be hit. I make up my mind not to resist, even if he beats me half to death.

But all my father can do is say in a composed voice, "You aren't going to get your tuition money from your sister now, young man. You'll just have to study hard and get into Tokyo University. The national universities are cheap and you have a good chance of getting a scholarship. But it's not going to be enough to study hard, you're going to have to study yourself into a breakdown. But then don't we all reap what we sow? Either you get into Tokyo, or you'll have to get a job. Unless you want to go to the Military Academy, but that's a different story."

I feel myself freeze, right to the guts. I turn my back to

my father and the rest of them and go out into the garden. It's a spring night. Underneath the dark sky, there's another rose-colored sky. They form a double stratum. Sultry steam and dust rise from the earth up to the skies and form a screen against the light, giving back a chaotic reflection of the lights from the homes all across Tokyo.

I've made myself a personal hideout where I sleep, in a shed at the far side of our little garden. It's like a bunk on a ship. There's no light, so when I close the door, I have to grope my way to bed. I made this bunk in the shed so I can get away from my family and be by myself. My bunk takes up only a third of the six-square-meter shed. The rest is piled high with junk.

I head for my bunk, groping my way through the junk. I touch one pile that's jumbled together between a desk and a chair. When I think of my bunk in the shed as a ship, this is the cabin. Useless as it is, I keep my eyes open in the dark. I open the desk drawer and take out a short-sword.

This is my weapon. I found it in the junk when I was building my bunk. It's only thirty centimeters long, but it has a Raikokuga inscription. I looked it up once in the library, and it seems Raikokuga was a swordsman in the late Muromachi period. That was four hundred years ago.

I unsheathe the sword and grasp it with both hands. With all my might I thrust it into the darkness between the piles of junk, again and again. It must be blood lust, a feeling that fills the shed and thrills my heart. Giving myself to my muffled cries, I pierce the darkness with my Raikokuga sword. The day will come when I'll stab the enemy to death with this Japanese sword. The enemy who I, like a man, will skewer.

That sudden realization comes to me with a premonition that's brimming with fierce confidence. But where is this enemy of mine? My enemy, is he my father? Is my enemy my sister? Or the American soldiers from the base? The men in the SDF? The Conservative politicians? Wherever my enemies are, I'll kill them. I'll kill them, I say with the same low cries.

As I slaughter my enemies, who cling as fast to me in the dark as the lice in the seams of my shirt, I gradually regain my composure. I even regret hurting my sister. If she goes blind because of what I did to her, I'll sacrifice my own eye to give her a corneal transplant. I have to pay for what I've done. Anybody who doesn't pay for his crimes with his own flesh and blood is a mean, despicable bastard. I'm not some trash who doesn't pay for what he does.

I shove the short-sword into the white wood sheath and put it back in the drawer. Groping my way, I get undressed and lie down on my bunk. Lying on my back in the dark, eyes open and ears strained, I have the feeling that the voices and shapes of all kinds of evil wilderness spirits are closing in on me. I feel like I'm at the bottom of a bowl, and my tiny nakedness is exposed to their ferocious attacks.

I hear the sounds of a record playing in the main house. Something by the Miles Davis Sextet. My brother is crazy about modern jazz. I remember how, during the whole episode of me kicking my sister and my old man making his contemptuous remarks, my brother was kneeling in the middle of all those pieces of plastic and tubes of glue he'd spread out on the tatami, and went right on putting together that model airplane, ignoring all of us. Like when a camera registers some detail the photographer hasn't noticed, I wasn't aware of it until now, but I discover that my brother's total lack of interest in us is neatly captured on the film of my memory. He's probably completely forgotten about the little storm that took place only ten minutes ago. He'll be there now, sitting in front of the record player, in raptures over his jazz, looking like a drug addict with his head wobbling on the end of his neck. Every few minutes he'll peel off another thin layer of the hardened glue that's stuck to the insides of his fingers, wondering whether he should've smacked me one, or maybe should've warned my sister not to get so carried away. The record player makes the bass and treble unnaturally loud, but to escape from his thoughts he turns the volume up another notch.

My brother was a genius, the hope of the family. Last year he graduated from the Liberal Arts Department of Tokyo University and got a job in a broadcasting company. At the university, my brother was a leader in his class. He worked like a maniac in the student festival. For the first few months after he joined the company he poured all his enthusiasm into his work as a producer on the special features team of a news program. He was doing a good job.

In those days I believed in my brother. I respected him.

Things I couldn't get from my old man, I got from my brother. But last summer he started complaining all the time about how tired he was. In autumn he took a week off. He went back to work after the holiday, but he was a changed man. He turned silent and polite, and developed a morbid fascination with modern jazz and a mania for building model airplanes. Since last fall, I haven't heard him say one word about his work, and I haven't heard him say anything about politics. Worse still, my brother, who used to be a passionate, confident, even eloquent speaker, hasn't talked to me about anything for as much as five minutes since the start of the year. Last winter, he broke a promise he made to climb the tough face of Mt. Tanigawa with me. That left a bitter taste.

I see him now listening to his modern jazz, with his washed-out body like a drunkard's, and much as I hate to admit it, I wouldn't want to take on the smallest slope with him as my partner. I have to ask, brother, how have you come to this?

Since my brother changed, I'm completely alone at home. A lonesome Seventeen. At this age, I should be growing and changing with the understanding of the people around me, but nobody makes the slightest effort to understand me, in spite of the fact that I'm in a real pinch . . .

Faintly, but unmistakably, something is signaling to me from outside the shed. I'd forgotten. I sit up in bed and open the round window I cut in the wall like a porthole in a ship's cabin. With an air of perfect composure the creature descends onto my cabin bed. Purring, it curls up on the blankets that cover my legs. This is Gangster, an alley cat that's always raising hell in the neighborhood. My father and mother are both stingy. They're the kind of people who tremble in fear at the thought that some pet animal might take the food out of their mouths. That means I can only keep pets that don't cause food problems. Last year I kept a colony of fifty ants in a jar, but they didn't make it through the winter. All I had left in my hands was the jar full of dirt, dug out in an amazing three-dimensional labyrinth. I was so sad I cried.

After that, I tamed Gangster. Gangster is a monster tomcat with tiger stripes. Since he's an alley cat, I don't have to worry about feeding him. He only comes home in the middle of the night to sleep, but it warms my heart that he came back this time when I was sunk in my own thoughts. I cluck my lips for him to come. Gangster pulls his heavy body up from the blankets on my legs and comes to drink my spittle. He's the only one who's celebrating my seventeenth birthday. The thought makes me sentimental. I push out a gob of spit with my tongue and let Gangster drink.

But Gangster is a real bastard, worse than Al Capone. He's not about to get sentimental or anything of the kind. Even while he's drinking my spit, he has his claws out far enough to dig into my chest, all the way through the blanket. He's getting a sure footing, so he's ready to make a getaway anytime he wants. I've never hugged Gangster. I can only leave it to him to come, and welcome him with my chest and knees. Even when he's purring, with his eyes closed and his wet nostrils quivering like a beautiful woman, he'll dash off in a mad rage if I pass my fingers over his body. Gangster doesn't want to be tied down. I understand that, but still I can't stand the way he goes back to the other end of the bed as soon as I run out of spit and my throat starts to get scratchy. It's like I'm falling into a pit of loneliness.

I want to hold Gangster's big tiger-striped body to stop his calm, composed departure from my chest. For one instant, Gangster and my hand meet with an intensity that sends off sparks. It's like the sparks from an electric-powered train. I lick the back of my hand where Gangster's claws have sliced open the flesh. I taste blood.

Gangster uses his head to send the porthole cover flying. He turns into a tiger-striped shark, dives into the stormy ocean, and disappears. The scratches hurt, but instead of getting mad at Gangster, I'm captured by admiration for him. He's a perfect villain: a barbarian, the incarnation of evil, ungrateful and shameless, explosive, a lone wolf. He trusts nobody, and steals whatever he wants. And still he's so dignified that he arouses a feeling of respect in me. As he walks in the dark, stalking his prey, he's as beautiful as an unwavering monument, but at the same time he's supple as rubber. When he glares at me I feel uneasy and apologetic. I even blush. Why hasn't he got even one weak spot? Once I watched in horror as he killed and ate a white cat in his secret hideaway, but even then he was splendid in his composure and dignity.

Kenzaburo Oe

I want to be a creature like Gangster, I think, but for that very reason I know it's a wish that can't come true without a miracle. The reason is that I have the weak brain of an albino pig in my head, and I'm self-conscious. As soon as I become conscious of myself, I feel the evil eyes of everybody in the world relentlessly staring at me. I move like a scarecrow. Every part of me revolts and starts to do exactly as it likes. I'm so ashamed I could die. The very fact that the sum of flesh and spirit which is me exists in this world makes me so ashamed that I want to die. It makes me wish I could live alone in a cave, like a Cro-Magnon man gone mad. It makes me want to put out the eyes of those others, or snuff myself out the same way.

Gangster wouldn't be conscious of himself. He probably thinks his body is nothing more than dirty skin, flesh, bone, and excrement, so he'd never blush in awkwardness if some other looked at him. I envy the dreams of that small brain in Gangster's big, solid head, spotted as it is with bald scars. A cat's nightmares would be at most an ash-gray haze, but the eeriness of my bad dreams is worse than juice laced with potassium cyanide.

My eyes are used to the dark, so I close them. I'm afraid of seeing ghosts in the shapes and shadows of the junk in my ship's cabin. With my eyes shut tight, I anxiously wait for the fear that sleep brings. It so happens that before I fall asleep, I'm captured by fear. It's the fear of death. I'm so afraid of death that I feel the need to vomit. Honestly, every time I feel this crushing fear of death, I get a sick feeling in my chest and have to throw up. The death I fear is like this: After this short life, I'll have to endure billions of years in unconsciousness, as a zero. This world, this universe, and all the other universes, will go on being for billions of years, and all that time I'll be a zero. For all eternity!

Every time I think about the endless progress of time after I die, I faint with fear. In my first physics class, the teacher talked about how there's an infinitely distant non-world, in other words, a place where nothing exists. A rocket flying straight out of this universe would go there, but eventually it'd find its way back. All the time it's disappearing straight into the distance, it's actually on its way back. While the physics teacher was explaining this, I fainted. Fear made me faint. I screamed, and I dirtied myself with piss and shit.

When I woke up there was shame, and hatred for my stinking self, and there was the unbearable look of the female students, but worst of all, I couldn't admit that what made me faint was the thought of nothingness and the infinity of physical space, which made me afraid of the eternity of time and the nothingness of my own mortal self. I desperately tried to make the teacher and my classmates think I'm epileptic.

Since then, I haven't had any real friends to whom I could open my heart. On top of that, my nightmares make me taste the fear of leaving all alone on a journey into that endless distance. The dead don't feel fear, because the dead aren't conscious. But in my dreams I wake up alone on a distant star, so I'm always conscious of fear. It's a sly invention of the dream distributor, full of evil intent.

Fear of death is closing in, bringing with it those nightmares. I struggle desperately to think about something else: WHEN I READ A NEWSPAPER ARTICLE ABOUT MICHIKO SHODA BEING CHOSEN CROWN PRINCESS, I THOUGHT MICHIKO WOULD GO TO A DISTANT STAR. I FELT OPPRESSED IN MY CHEST AND WEPT. I TREMBLED WITH FEAR. WHY WAS THAT? I WAS AFRAID MICHIKO WOULD DIE. I TAPED MICHIKO'S PICTURE TO THE WALL AND PRAYED THE MARRIAGE WOULD FAIL. IT WASN'T JEALOUSY. WHEN I SAW A YOUNGSTER THROW A STONE ON TV, AGAIN I FELT OPPRESSED AND WEPT. APPARENTLY THAT YOUNGSTER TOO HAD A PICTURE OF MICHIKO IN HIS CLOSET. THAT NIGHT I HAD A DREAM IN WHICH I WAS BOTH MICHIKO AND THE STONE-THROWING YOUNGSTER. WHY WAS THAT?

Why was that? I can't escape the fear of death. I raise myself and open my eyes. I clutch my trembling body and peer into the dark. Today, the fear is the worst it's ever been. I break out in a greasy sweat. I wish, I very nearly pray, that I can get married as soon as possible. My wife doesn't have to be a beauty, but she has to have true compassion. She has to stay up and watch over me at night to make sure I don't die in my sleep.

How can I ever escape from this fear? It hits me, how

good it would be if, after I die, I could be one branch of a big tree. I would wither, but not perish, since the big tree, me included, would continue to exist. Then I wouldn't have to feel the fear of death. But I am all alone in this world. I'm insecure and frightened. I doubt everything in this world. I can't really understand a thing. I feel like it's all beyond my grasp. I feel like this world belongs to the others. I don't have the freedom to do anything. I have no friends, no buddies. Should I become a left-winger and join the Communist party? Would that solve my loneliness?

Then again, I've just been saying all the things the big shots in the left wing say, and I was routed by my sister, who's nothing but a nurse. I know I can't grasp the world the way the Left grasps it. The plain truth is, I don't understand a thing. I don't have what it takes to find a giant oak that can stand up to the snow and wind of eternity and will take me on as one small branch.

As long as I can't understand, and I still have these dregs of insecurity stagnating in my head, it won't make any difference if I join the Communists. I'll still be insecure, and won't be able to believe. What's worse, it's not likely I'd be accepted as a comrade by the Communists. Me, a dwarf who was squelched by his nearsighted sister who works at an SDF hospital.

If only this world would offer me a hand I could grasp with passion, in simplicity and trust! I feel weak. I give in. I fall back into my cabin bed and grope around under the blankets. When my fingers take hold of my sex, they force it into an erection so I can masturbate. Tomorrow I have the achievement tests for the university entrance exams and the physical education trials. If I masturbate for a second time today, I'm going to be exhausted tomorrow and running the eight hundred meters will be an absolute fiasco. Tomorrow fills me with an indefinable dread, but masturbation is the only escape, however brief, from a night of fear.

The night of a city of others is moaning outside the shed. The essence of spring is being worn away by the dirty city air, but it comes out of the sultry, fragrant beech wood in the far distance to stir my flesh and blood and sweep me away into a sea of insecurity. I am seventeen years old, a poor sad Seventeen. Happy birthday, happy birthday, fumble with that crotch and go ahead and do you-know-what.

I need to imagine something obscene. I think of my mother and father, moaning and groaning as they do it. Their assholes are both stark naked. I imagine their pleasure as they fondle each other in the warm, fetid air under the quilts. Suddenly I doubt that I am actually the child of my old man's sperm. Maybe I was born out of my mother's infidelity. I wonder if maybe my father knows, and that's why he's so coldhearted.

But my orgasm is approaching. Peach flowers bloom everywhere around me, hot springs bubble up, the giant lights of Las Vegas glitter. The fear and doubt, the insecurity, the sadness and misery, that all dissolves now. What bliss it would be if my whole life were one long orgasm. If only it were always, always an orgasm!

My ejaculation wets my crotch. Still panting, I discover once more in the darkness of my shed the birthday of a poor, sad Seventeen. Dispirited and bitter, I start to sob.

2

I'm not feeling very good when I wake up. My head aches, my arms are heavy, my legs are heavy, my whole body feels slightly feverish. I feel like every other in the world has come to inform my newly awakened body of the fact that I'm an impotent good-for-nothing.

I have a premonition that something bad is going to happen today. Until last year, I'd made up my mind to develop one new habit for each birthday. But my seventeenth birthday doesn't make me want to do anything new at all. At seventeen, I'm already going downhill. Some people start downhill at fifty, and some keep on the upside until they're sixty. But I have the sobering feeling that uphill was already over for me yesterday.

The realization that I'm sinking myself in the quagmire of gloom from the minute I open my eyes robs me of the strength to get up. I lie in bed without moving, with my eyes open, in the warmth of the blankets. No matter how lousy I felt, no matter what pain-in-the-ass job I was stuck with, until last year, at least in the moment when I opened my eyes in the morning, I could feel a warm lump of happiness in my breast. I loved the morning. I felt like that lump in my chest was urging me to dash out the door, like I had to say hello to the morning world. I could smile in sympathy and accept the unaccountably sunny cries of the morning-radio exercise instructor. Why? Because it was morning. It made me want to call out, "Aren't you bubbling with hope and happiness too, because it's morning?"

But now, the junior high student next door, who'd go along with anything with a smile on his face, has the radio blasting away at full volume. When I hear the arrogant, put-on voice on the radio cheering me on, it only fills me with irritation and anger. Nobody has the right to call out the count for anybody else. That's what I like to tell him.

Rays of sunlight shine through the doors and the wall and the cracks in the roof, giving a golden color to the dusty saddle of the child's bicycle. The bicycle of my happy childhood. Once when I was riding in the roller-skating rink in the park, a foreign woman chased after me, wanting to take my picture. While I was resting, with the bike parked against the wisteria trellis, that oversized blond woman suddenly materialized from behind me. She pressed her cheek against the bicycle saddle and smiled at me with a face that had turned crimson. I was as embarrassed as if she'd touched my bare buttocks, and ran home, leaving my bike standing there. But the woman's crazy laughter followed me, rising and falling in what sounded like convulsive spasms. After I started to learn English, I recalled what that giant woman had screamed at me. I remembered because I was so terrified.

"Oh pretty little boy. Please come back! Pretty little boy."

SEVENTEEN

I was a pretty little boy. The days of childhood, when my heart could pound with that kind of happiness, are over, but I really was a pretty little boy. I felt good, everybody in the world was happy, the entire cosmos felt good as it turned around the sun. But forget about the cosmos. Dark shoots of evil are all I find now in this tiny shed, and even in my own body. Signs of constipation, headache, like the grinding and scratching of sand that's found its way into my every joint, so many grains for each spot. As I lie here with blanket pulled over me, I sink deeper and deeper into this black mood. But hiding and crying under my blanket isn't going to make me feel any better, not without some kind of miracle. Because outside this shed, all the others in the world were up early and working hard at ruining my mood.

Just give up on the whole business, I think. I yawn as I crawl down from my bed. My eyes are wet with what I guess you'd call transparent muck. I don't know if it's tears or some other fluid. I hang my head as I pull up my trousers. My sex has shrunken in on itself and sits small and quiet, like a fat sparrow crouching on a cold roof. It gives me a certain masochistic pleasure to see how impotent it looks, even in the morning. I can almost see myself at the age of forty, with my pants down around my knees, showing my impotent little potato to the psychologist: "I had the first symptoms on my seventeenth birthday. Yes sir. Done too much of that, hadn't I . . ."

I pick up signs that my sister and my old man are leaving the house, talking in tones that sound like they're arguing about something. My sister's voice is sullen, but my father, level-headed and nasty in his superiority, speaks in a balmy voice. But the old man's mood is definitely not balmy. He's trying to put on the voice of American individualism.

At any rate, I'm relieved to know that I didn't blind my sister. What's more, I can get by without seeing her this morning. I'm always too worried about things. I imagine the worst possible outcome in every situation and every time somebody's sick. But I've never gotten myself into anything I couldn't get myself out of. I'm not the type of man to really do anything. I'm a man who can't even kick out his sister's eye. I'm the kind of man who ends up repenting, and feels relieved to be saved. I'm a man who can't do the slightest thing to change the real world. I'm the man who can't. I am an impotent Seventeen. To tell you the one thing I can do, all I can do is escape from the eyes of other people, hide, and masturbate. The ones who're recreating and shoring up the world like so many architects are all the others. While I'm locked up in this shed I call a ship's cabin doing you-know-what, all those others are monkeying around with the world and saying, "Yes, this is it!" Especially when it comes to politics. That's a job for them, beginning to end. Even when I'm marching in a demonstration, I'm always alone inside, thinking it's all a waste of time. There's no chance that I'm going to have any effect on politics, so I know that kind of thing is completely pointless. And the politicians are others even among the others. They do their politics in the Diet and the tea-houses, just clapping their hands and saying, "Yes, this is it!"

That's politics.

When I turn twenty, I'll cast my vote in the trash can. You'll see me dead before you'll see me in a voting booth.

The ideas my sister brandished last night seem to fit the real me a lot better than the opinions I was screaming out in every direction. I boil over with a shame that turns my flesh and blood to gall. After all, I am an idiot who doesn't know the first thing about politics. I don't have a single idea of my own. I'd do just as well if I were a speechless chimpanzee doing nothing but you-know-what.

Again I feel a masochistic pleasure. It's like I enjoy the horrible things done to me by others.

"Oh, Carol!" I sing as I go out of the shed. Out, under a dazzlingly clear blue sky, into the shining world of others.

As I go out, this is what I sing: *You hurt me, and you made me cry. But if you leave me, I will surely die. Oh, oh, Carol, you treat me cruel!*

～

I'm twenty minutes late for school. To make matters worse, the achievement test has already started. Willy-nilly, I pick up the question and answer sheets and sit down at a desk in the very back row. As I sit, I sneak a look at the guy beside me. The bastard's answer sheet is already a quarter full. The penciled letters march together in close rows, like the footprints of lead soldiers. When I think about what a handicap it is to be late for an exam, I'd like to murder the bunch of bastards who show up early and sit calmly at their desks, with their pencils sharpened and ready.

It's the Japanese test. I read the questions, but I'm in such a panic that not one thing comes to me. Instead, the blood comes rushing to my head, practically boiling over. I'm seized with fear as I read, and then reread the questions. I try to concentrate, but other things come bubbling up into my head, and I can't think properly.

The moon was sinking over the hills in a crystal-clear sky, the wind was very cold, and the voices of the insects in the grass brought to her the urge. She found it really difficult to get up and leave these grasses. Even though the crickets cry themselves into exhaustion, my tears still fall until the long night ends. Still she was reluctant to get under way. In the reeds where the insects are singing incessantly, the person from above the clouds sprinkles the dew. Complaints are about to be uttered.

What work is this from, and by whom? Surely it has to be the *Tale of Genji*, by Murasaki Shikibu, but I'm not confident. "Brought to her the urge," I think, but to do what? I don't have any idea.

Urge sounds erotic, I think. Suddenly I fall into a lewd fantasy. In a magazine I was reading in a bookstore sometime or another, I recall that there was a woman called

Sasanoha Ogin, in ancient times, and she definitely said to some wandering samurai, I've got the urge.

There's a couplet in the quotation, but is it by one person or not? I put the dialogue in quotation marks. Still, the phrase "In the reeds where the insects are singing incessantly, the person from above the clouds sprinkles the dew," reminds me of the wet feeling in my crotch after I abuse myself. I'm a feeble-minded sex maniac.

I've only finished a third of the test when the bell rings.

"Dead out!" I mutter, trying to pass it off as a joke. To my surprise, it hits like lead in the pit of my stomach. I almost forget to write my name.

The classroom is a disgusting sight after the test. They've all written their answers with such enthusiasm, without once taking their eyes off the page, and now their cheeks are flushed and they're bleary-eyed. They have the obscene expression of kids who've just finished a petting session. They're either feverishly excited, or else utterly dejected. I'm one of the utterly dejected. They form into groups, each according to his taste, and start talking about the exam results. But even then I stay in my chair. My head droops like I've had the stuffings knocked out of me.

The honor students crowd together in their own little group, talking in cool tones. Until last year I belonged to that group, but now I don't have the courage to join them. Still, I prick up my ears and try to catch what they're saying. The honor students are in the know about everything. They've got their ways of sniffing out the teachers' plans.

They talk with the despicable complacency of technicians—technicians in getting good grades. They're arrogant and full of virtue, and don't have the least interest in the likes of me.

"*Kiritsubo* was a long shot," they're saying. "I thought they'd serve up something laced with classical Chinese. I was betting on the *Great Mirror* or something like that."

But, of course, that type has turned in perfect answers.

"I heard they're putting together a special class for Tokyo University if you average over 85 on the next test. I'm out for that."

"Mr. Modesty, aren't you? If you don't make it, there won't be anybody in the Tokyo class."

The honor students make me want to puke. At the same time, I remember what my old man said last night. I have the despairing feeling that I've been driven into a corner. I don't stand a chance of getting into the Tokyo course. Those bastards are going to be studying with the chosen ones, with all the grace and good fortune of high-society American bridegrooms, while I'm left to fight a losing struggle in a low-level class, where the teachers don't make any effort to teach.

"Still, they were good questions. Above the average, I must say."

"But as something out of *Genji*, wasn't it too standard? The real battle won't be like that. It would've been simple enough to make a more complicated question about court ladies' language. If you add the next line in the paragraph, it gets confusing, and you can't tell who the polite language is meant for."

"Oh, it's the real battle, is it? It sounds like you're already on your way to Tokyo."

"Don't make me laugh! I'm talking about the entrance exam for prep school."

They make me want to vomit. I'm so angry I feel like I could throw up. Those bastards are so happy they're actually licking their chops over what's left of the excitement from the exam.

There's also a group of different, more straightforward people. They're getting laughs from the people around them, especially the girls. One comedian is roaring away in an amazingly loud voice.

"Me, now, I thought she was feeling the urge to piss. See, during the Heian Era, they didn't have public toilets, now did they? So, you see, she just couldn't hold it anymore, and she sprinkled the dew in the reeds where the crickets were singing."

Everybody laughs at this. The boy is smart, but he's strange, and he acts like he's constantly aware of the fact. His nickname is Shintoho, after a film company that specializes in soft-core pornography. He refuses to watch anything else, and goes out to the suburbs, or even to Chiba Prefecture to catch the Triple Feature Week when they're showing erotic-grotesque films.

"And what about 'complaints are about to be uttered,' Shintoho?"

The girl who asks this sounds like she's interested in him. She giggles as she waits for some ludicrous answer.

"The cop on the beat had complained. You see, she'd violated the Minor Offenses Act."

"So they had beat cops in the Heian Era, Shintoho?"

"You're really a green one," our hero says. "But let me tell you the true story. In fact she's trying to fool him about the sound, saying 'it seems that the long-horned beetles are crying.' Then she wipes herself."

"My God, what a pervert," the girl squeals, writhing with lascivious excitement. She runs out of the room, and our hero is swamped with applause. He raises his hands as though he wants to quiet the crowd, but actually he's following the model of a popular American TV-show host. He's in high spirits.

Still, at least he must have understood the question more deeply and accurately than I did. With that thought, I'm completely knocked out. Suddenly I can't stand to sit here by myself. I see myself standing on a narrow path of crumbling sand, between the abyss of insecurity and the abyss of impotence. I leave my seat, but I don't have the courage to go near the group of honor students. But when Shintoho makes a gesture inviting me into his group, I feel like I'm being unfairly treated, as an inferior being. I feel insulted. I turn my back on this popular entertainer and leave the classroom.

As soon as I do, I'm sorry. I see that I'm narrow-minded, and fall into self-loathing. I really am alone and insecure, as helpless and easily hurt as a crab that's just changed into a soft new shell.

Seventeen

When the bell rings again, I have to go back to the class-room. This time it's the mathematics test. The mere thought of it makes me tremble with fear. My math answers are even worse than my disgraceful performance in Japanese. I listen to the bell signaling the end of the period in a daze. I feel like I want to cry. But when I think about what's coming this afternoon, I realize that bad as it was, this morning was actually the easy part.

~

The test of general physical ability is held in the afternoon. Physical education is my worst subject. When I think about my body, it stops me in my tracks. The thought of having an erection while I'm wearing nothing but my gym shorts makes me tremble with shame. Practically paralyzed with fear, I have to run the eight hundred meters. And I have to do it on the big sports field, in full view of the female students and everybody on the street!

The big field is behind the school building. It faces a shopping street across a strip of pavement. Adults and kids with time to kill lean on the low fence and watch the field. They aren't there to appreciate the beauty and power of sports. They gather only to enjoy themselves by laughing at and ridiculing the pratfalls of the students. They can laugh at the agony we endure when the coach makes us run. For that one moment they can smile and forget the contemptuous and demanding ways in which they are treated by their company bosses and customers.

Kenzaburo Oe

We boys are gathered in the middle of the track on the big sports field. As we do our warm-ups, we wait for the physical education director to come out of his office with his stopwatch and his little black book. We're like a noisy herd of cattle, some of us scared, some of us brimming with courage, some like cats enjoying the late spring sunshine, lazing, without a thought in our heads. The honor students are debilitated from studying for their entrance exams. They're blinded and confused by the light. You can see that they're terrified by the long distance they have to run. They look pale. But I think it'll be easier for them to get through this grueling, humiliating race than for me, since the clique they belong to knows they're a bunch of worn-out book-worms.

Then we have the track stars, who're so full of energy they take it on themselves to call time for the warm-ups. One in particular holds a whole handful of the year's best city records. His attitude is even worse than what the honor students showed in class. He stops his jumping for a second, shakes his head over his ankle, and then goes back to jumping twice as high as anybody else. It's all a big act, but it's enough to make me pretty jealous. It pricks my feeling of inferiority.

Some guys are just lazing in the sunshine, not putting any effort into their warm-ups. In class they were the same. They look down on their own abilities, so it doesn't bother them to be looked at. They have the shameless-ness of dilettantes.

I'm not like anybody else in my class. I am alone, and probably more frightened than anyone. I only hope it's over soon. I try not to think about it too much.

The small field bulges like a tumor from the larger field, in the space between the school buildings. The girls are playing volleyball there. They're wearing headbands and ungainly bloomers that make them look like ducks. Several girls are standing at the side of the court, still dressed in their skirts, watching the game with the fixed, dull-witted look of sick animals. They're menstruating, I think with contempt. That's a public secret, and everybody knows.

Every week, Shintoho enthusiastically notes the names of the girls who watch from the sidelines. He keeps a chart of the menstrual cycles of every girl in school. He knows who's safe according to the Ogino rhythm method, and he makes a point of telling them what days they can do it. "I'm available any time," he adds to everybody, "so if you've made up your mind to get rid of that treasure, just give me a call." He's built himself quite a reputation that way. The girls don't hate him for it, and it makes him popular with the boys.

If I did anything with a girl, I'd be an outcast from the very next day. I wouldn't have the courage to show my face at school. Why is it that only he can get by with anything he wants to do? And he's the only guy in our class with experience. He's like the devil in a play I saw when I was a child, thanks to the church Sunday Club. God and man have to suffer, work, and repent, while the devil alone lounges around, shouting obscenities, profanities, and lies as he enjoys the banquet.

How I'd like to play the devil's part!

But what on earth would be the devil's part in times like these? What kind of job would he get after graduation? I think about this, panting for breath from doing my warm-ups. Would that be the devil's job in this present society that is so incomprehensible to me . . . for example, the job of poisoner-devil?

As usual, that Shintoho is entertaining everybody in sight. "Damn, but I'm in a mess. The nuclear test in Nevada last week must've caused a disruption. I'm going to have to revise my charts. Or maybe Miss Emiko Sugi is suffering diarrhea."

I listen hard and give a quick look at the small sports field, like almost all the other boys. A large, white face that's just like Sugi is looking our way. Of all the gloomy, skirt-wearing girls, only Sugi is looking at us, with her head held high. My chest feels warm. I release my hot breath in time to the sighing of all the other boys.

Each class has its queen. She's not only beautiful, but also possesses an overwhelming dignity and a coquettish charm. She's the envy of all the other girls, and drives the boys crazy. Sugi is the queen of our class. I'm one of the poor devils who writes love letters to her, and then tears them up before he gets up the courage to give them to her. With Sugi staring at me, I feel all over again the pain of the sad figure I cut. If she were a girl in bloomers and I could find the audacity to stare back at her fat white thighs, I might get the best of my shame. But a girl firmly wrapped in a skirt doesn't have a weak point anywhere. There's nothing I can take advantage of to make her wince, and let me transform myself from the watched into the watcher. Still, it's that Sugi . . .

"Why do you think Miss Emiko Sugi is so interested in us?" Shintoho asks. His feeling of triumph makes his repulsive, pimple-swollen face shine like the sun. To give me the final blow, he cries out, "I tossed a mystery note into that girl's desk. Guys who jerk off fall flat as soon as they start, so she'll know right away. At this very minute, Miss Sugi is about to discover a *Kinsey Report* fact of human life. Abstainers! Don't give up!"

The physical education teacher comes galloping over to put a stop to the commotion. Then the test starts, the eight-hundred-meter run. We're supposed to do two laps around the four-hundred-meter track in groups of ten. The starting line is on the side away from the small field, which lets us start and finish as far as possible from the girls, but it puts us right under the noses of the bunch who're watching from the street. As soon as the test begins and the first group starts running, the eager audience swarms to the starting line. They sit themselves on the fence and get ready to watch our down-home horse race.

I stand at the starting line. Lanes are drawn in lime on the sun-baked ground. They look like they go on forever. The starting gun sounds. When I start running, jostling against the bare arms of the boys beside me, I trip, and before long my chest aches and I'm panting. From the start, the runners sprint with incredible, cold-blooded speed. Life is hell, I think, and I'm a slave, gasping for air with the devil forcing me on. He's dressed in spotless training pants and a baseball cap, and he clutches a starter's pistol in his hand. I run without a clue, trying to escape this hellish world, but there's no way out.

Before long the other runners have left me behind. Far in back, I run alone. My legs are heavy, like in bad dreams when I'm chased by a monster. My brain feels like it's on fire. I realize that I'm groaning out loud as I run. When I pass the girls I force myself to run by the book, chest thrown out, head held high, knees up, but the effort back-fires as soon as I try it. I can't thrust out my chin or swing my arms. My wrists dangle below my waist, and I can barely drag my feet along the ground. I stagger along, groaning one long, unbroken groan. Still, I finish the first four hundred meters. When I make it back to the starting line, I try to show a smiling face to the other boys who're waiting their turn, pretending everything's fine, but the skin of my face is thick and stiff and refuses to move. All I can manage is a sad pout, with only my eyes moving in an aimless stare.

"You!" the coach roars. "Act like a man. And stop that pigeon-toed dog-trot!"

From the street a child's voice follows me.

"Look how white he is! He must be sick!"

That's how slow I'm running. Everybody is watching

my sad, farcical stumbling. All the others in the world stare at the filthy Seventeen as he runs his pigeon-toed dog-trot with his jaundiced lips and tears of agony pouring down his pallid cheeks. They smile with derision.

The Others are neat, dry, and gallantly composed. I am a disgrace. I'm dizzy and mawkish, awkwardly frightened, puffy fat, and reeking of sweat like I'm rotting away even as I run this miserable race. The others slobber on themselves like dogs, they puff out their bellies as they watch me, but I know that what they really see is the naked me, the me that's red-faced and trembling with fear, me addicted to obscene fantasies, me masturbating, me anxious, the me who's a coward and liar. As the Others look at me and laugh, they scream out, "We know all about you. You're done in by the poison of self-consciousness, done in by your budding sexual desires. You're rotting away from the inside. We can see all the way through to your indecent fetid crotch! You're nothing but a lonely gorilla, masturbating in front of our very eyes!"

I've made it to the six-hundred-meter mark, and now the girls are watching me again. I pray that I'll have a heart attack and die, but that kind of miracle doesn't happen. Instead, I finally have to accept the fact that my wide-awake self-consciousness roars like a bear in a heat of shame.

I stagger across the finish line a good hundred meters behind the other runners. Just as my pathetic relief at finishing the race dampens my breast with a liquid warmth, the coach smiles a wry smile and points behind me. I think I'm not going to smile, but I look back, wearing a vague little grin, and discover the long black trail I've made by pissing in my pants.

Like a storm in a forest, the sneering laughter of a whole world of Others howls around me! I've finished this ugly eight-hundred-meter race in utter desperation, giving it every atom of sincerity I possess, and this is the cruel welcome I receive. I may be a poor, ugly Seventeen, but the world of Others has treated me with cruelty, with more cruelty than even I deserve.

The coldness of my wet pants makes me sneeze. In total exhaustion, I sink into the pit of shame. I make up my mind to stop hanging on and trying to find some good in this world of Others. Why? Probably because if I don't kindle an enemy spirit, if I don't rake up hatred for them, I'm afraid I'm going to break down and cry.

3

I'm alone, waiting for the train. There was a student council meeting after the physical education trials, but I didn't have the courage to go.

A voice calls out from behind me. "Hey, you want to come along and be a Sakura for the right-wingers? They need an audience to make them look good, you know."

I turn around to see Shintoho approaching me. His face is serious. He must think I'm going to punch him or something, the way he shrinks back for a moment, but then he spills out a flood of words that loosens me up.

"Don't get mad, man. I didn't feel like going to that stupid meeting either, you know. I happened to see you at the ticket gate, so I came after you. You really have guts, you know. I changed my mind about you. What you did I could never have done. Coaches are bastards anyway, but that one's the worst. We aren't horses, are we? Why would we want to run eight hundred meters? But he makes us, that tyrant. People are saying he's pissed off because that good-looking music teacher dumped him. I got pretty sick of it too, running like that. Everybody was happy when you pissed. We should've all pissed. That would've put that dictator in his place."

Shintoho realizes that his talk is getting on my nerves.

"There's this rightist group," he says. "I sometimes go to see what they're up to. They give speeches from a platform in the square in front of Shinbashi Station. That's why they need Sakura. Those in school uniforms are especially good. You get ¥500 a day for it. What do you say? You want to be a Sakura? I'm not kidding, you know."

Shintoho must be intimidated by me. It's the first time I've ever seen him make such a serious face, or heard him make such an earnest plea. When I don't answer, half out of doubt about whether to believe him, he starts giving me his personal history.

"Me, I'm not exactly what you'd call a right-winger. I'm more of an anarchist, a new kind of anarchist like the beatniks. Still, it makes me mad to hear the progressive parties and the Communists bad-mouthing the SDF. You once defended the SDF yourself, didn't you? You said your sister was an SDF nurse. I liked that. I'm a coward, so I didn't say anything about it, but actually my old man is in the SDF too. He's a colonel in the infantry. That's why I'd like to smash the progressives and the Commies. If the Right wants to do that for me, then the Right gets my support. So, sometimes I do drop in on them. You've probably heard of the Imperial Way Party. The boss is Kunihiko Sakakibara. During the war he was in a special brigade in Mukden. Nobody in Japan tells him what to do. Since the war in Manchuria, he's been a personal friend of Prime Minister Oka."

Shintoho is obviously a lot more naive than I thought. The naive Shintoho is after all a complete nobody. I lighten up. A feeling of superiority flits past me like a bird. I catch it and don't let go.

Just then the train rolls in. I give Shintoho a nod, and we get on the train together. I couldn't stand to go home and be alone. Being with somebody for whom I feel nothing but contempt seems safer for my wounded pride than being by myself. I can relax now. It's like escaping from your insecurity by getting drunk on cheap booze.

After we're on the train, Shintoho's attitude changes completely. He sinks into a dead silence. Apparently he's going to treat the fact that we're going to be Sakura at a right-wing speech with secrecy worthy of a nuclear spy. Maybe he's even convinced that this is just as important. The bullshit artist Shintoho probably hasn't ever told anybody that he's mixed up in some right-wing group. If he did, half the student body would know about it by tomorrow.

The movement of the train bounces us around to the point where I actually feel my chest touching Shintoho's pimply chest. His filthy hair, where the dirt seems to be kneaded together with pomade, touches my chin. It makes me realize that I'm a lot taller than Shintoho. I'd never noticed before. Odd as it may seem, the realization cheers me from the depths of my heart. We stay like this, silently rubbing chests, all the way to Shinbashi Station.

The platform is strangely deserted for a station in the city at three in the afternoon. As I walk along, my shoulders and arms touching Shintoho's, I suddenly feel like I'm an accomplice in some sexual adventure. Later I will often recall this occasion. An event of the utmost importance for the future direction of my life is crystallizing before my very eyes. At least, that's the profound feeling I have, here in Shinbashi Station on this late spring afternoon. An old railway employee is sweeping the platform with an old-fashioned bamboo broom. With his rational outsider's eyes, that must be how he sees us: a couple of high school students, pale-faced and pimply, on our way to some sexual prank.

The speech by Kunihiko Sakakibara of the Imperial Way Party is a disaster. That much is clear, as soon as I enter the square where he's speaking. Not a soul is paying any real attention to the raging old lunatic on the platform. He simply goes on raving, incoherent and alone, like he doesn't expect anybody to listen. Maybe Sakakibara wants to be the first man in history to stand up, single-handedly, to the noise of the incoming trains at Shinbashi. As he screams away he's not even looking at the audience. He's gazing at the trains on the elevated tracks. Sakura like me and Shintoho are supposed to clap and cheer, but the imperturbable Sakakibara doesn't give us a chance, so we just hang around. The roaring human lion with the dangerous look on his face seems to have completely forgotten about the Sakura he hired. From behind the backs of some irresponsible bystanders, me and Shintoho, more out of curiosity than anything else, are observing the lunatic. That a man can be as dignified and aggressive as a trooper while he's roaring like this against the ridicule and indifference of so many others, is a startling concept. The platform where he's speaking doesn't give him as much as one decoration to protect his flanks. There's only a single Japanese flag, dangling lifelessly from its bamboo pole. On the two sides of the platform stand young men in black shirts and armbands, and some older men in suits. But even they seem to be more interested in the horse race bulletin board on the opposite side of the square than in Kunihiko Sakakibara. Probably they've got money riding on a horse named Imperial Way, in hopes of winning the big one.

Then one of the other Sakura develops a new enthusiasm for his work. He's a remarkably skinny, dreary man with a stoop. Clasping his knees, he's sitting in the middle of the concrete benches that face the platform. Sakakibara has to stop for a minute to push a little spittle into his over-worked throat. As he does, he stares into space as if the forced interruption in his ravings fills his heart with regret. During that brief moment, the Sakura breaks into wild applause and shouts of encouragement. This single person's frenzy attracts the attention of some others who're loafing around like they've sworn on their old man's dying bed to never get involved in anything and never abandon the position of onlooker. They circle around, looking for some kind of scandal. Me and Shintoho hurry toward the center of the square before the circle closes, and grab a seat on the last bench. After all, we're Sakura.

It's clear to me though that Shintoho is nothing more than another unenthusiastic Sakura himself. It's just talk when he says he drops in on the Imperial Way people. If he were a member, he wouldn't be so timid and quiet.

When we sit down one look around tells me that the twenty-odd men sitting in front of us, just like the model Sakura who's in the middle clapping and cheering, were all hired by the Imperial Way. They all look and act like day-laborers, sitting there not knowing what to do with their hands. It looks like they're expecting somebody to dump a cat in their laps. As the man in the middle of the circle claps more and more fanatically they stir, ill at ease and with a tense, sad expression.

I glance at Shintoho to see whether he's going to start clapping. That confuses him. He hurries to explain that the men are all hired Sakura, like us. "Today the weather's good, but Sakakibara likes to hold meetings on rainy days, since it's easier to mobilize the out-of-work day-laborers. Then he can say things like, 'When Sakakibara speaks, even the heavens are moved by his loyalty. The raindrops are tears lamenting the end of the world.' Or 'Sakakibara is the rain man of devotion.' People who are sheltering themselves from the rain don't get mad about that. Sometimes they even appreciate it."

That sounds believable. Rain makes people susceptible. Me especially. When it rains, or on humid days or when the atmospheric pressure is low, my body feels fit, and I want to do things for people.

"Besides," Shintoho goes on, "the day-laborers who're out of work because of the rain are happy. It's not hard work. All they have to do is keep quiet and listen, and clap once in a while."

He adds this in a defensive tone, like he thinks I doubt him. I know I'm putting him under pressure. I'm not depressed now. At least for this brief moment I feel like I'm free from the shameful memory of what happened on the sports field. When night comes, I'll tremble with shame, so much that I'll want to kill myself, but for now at least I have a stay of execution.

The day-laborers who're sitting on the bench staring at the hands in their laps also look like they've had a stay of execution from something. The looks of passersby pierce their heads, their backs and shoulders, like a thousand arrows. The afternoon sunlight of late spring is receding like an ebb tide, and a feeling of despair, chilly as a winter night, mingles with the sunlight. Tokyo the metropolis abandons all hope and is crushed by exhaustion. Only the one workaholic Sakura, with his manic applause and cheers, doesn't forsake the cause.

On stage Kunihiko Sakakibara is still ranting and raving. His hoarse voice, defying gravity, flees into the sky above us. Men with too much time on their hands have collected around the fringes of the square. Their cold hawk-like mockery takes aim on him. I slowly sink into a kind of daydream. My ears perceive the deafening noise of the city as an enormous medley, not as separate voices and sounds. This din, like the warm, heavy sea on a summer night, cuts my tired body off from reality and lets it float. I forget the idle people behind me, forget Shintoho, forget the day-laborers, forget the screaming Sakakibara. I am like a single grain of sand in the desert of the city. With a gentleness filled with a serenity I've never experienced before, I forgive my petty and worn-out self. My hostility and hate I turn solely on the real world, solely on the Others. Always I've been blaming myself, always attacking my weaknesses and covering them with the mud of self-loathing, always thinking there was no one more deserving of hate.

But the critic inside me has suddenly disappeared from my heart. I am pampering my injured self by licking and nursing my plentiful wounds. I am a puppy, and at the same time, I'm the mother dog, blinded by affection. Unconditionally I forgive myself. I nurse myself, the puppy. And equally unconditionally, I bark and bite at the others who treat me, the puppy, with cruelty. I'm doing this in a sleepy, dazed state of mind. Before long, like it's a dream, my ears start to pick up the words of malice and hate which I myself am slinging at the others of the real world. In fact, it is Sakakibara who's speaking these words, but his expressions of malice and hate are exactly the same as those in my own heart. Sakakibara is my soul screaming. The sensation makes me shiver. Then, with all the strength in my body, I start to listen and take in his cries.

"Those damned shit heads. Those petty officials. Infamous pimps selling their own country, that's what they are. Isn't it unbelievable that they dare to build houses and have wives and children on Japan's sacred soil? They don't deserve the name Japanese. They belong in some beastly country like the Soviet Union or Communist China. I won't stop them from going there, I'll kick their asses. Those bastards are so busy having their buttholes cleaned out by that faggot Khrushchev, they don't even have time to fart. They plan to use the dirty money they've collected through strikes and demagoguery to bribe that barbarian Mao Tse Tung. And then in less than two years they themselves will be purged for right-wing deviations. They'll be forced into self-criticism, and their heads will roll. That's what they deserve. They call us a violent mob, but ladies and gentlemen, think about it: They're the ones who earn their living with mob violence, with demonstrations and strikes and sit-ins. Who's been responsible for more terrorism in modern times? The

Right, or the Left? I ask you. Those Red pigs carry out a massacre and nobody says a word. The concentration camps weren't just a Nazi thing. The Russians have them too, and even worse!

"Their people go to China, and they're treated to banquets with money extracted from the people's blood, sweat, and tears. And then they apologize. In the name of the Imperial people of Japan, they apologize! Forgive us, they say, for the genocide caused by Japanese militarism, for the so-called Sanko Strategy, with its killing and burning and even more horrible crimes. Our friends, the veterans from Manchuria, were crying with fury. They wanted to see those bastards' wives raped and murdered. Those traitors, shameless bootlickers, fork-tongued and irresponsible, murderers, imposters, adulterers. It's nauseating. I hereby vow to you: I'll kill them, I'll slaughter them, I'll rape their wives and daughters, I'll feed their sons to the pigs. Such is Justice. Such is my duty. Extermination, that's the divine will laid upon my shoulders at birth. I'll throw them into hell. There's no other way for us to survive, but to burn them at the stake. We throw THEM into hell so WE can live!

"We're weak, and only by exterminating them will we survive. Those are the words their pal, their god Lenin proclaimed. Ladies and gentlemen, we will kill them to the last man to protect our own weak lives. Such is Justice!" The cruel symphony of malice and hate is resounding throughout the world loud enough to destroy the amplifier. "We will kill them to the last man to protect our own weak lives. Such is Justice!"

Kenzaburo Oe

I stand and clap. I cheer. The leader on stage is reflected in my hysterical eyes as a radiant golden being appearing from the darkness. I keep on clapping and cheering. Such is Justice! For the cruelly treated, for the wounded weak soul. Such is Justice!

"That one, he's a Rightist, and he's still so young. Look. He's a real pro."

I turn around suddenly to face the group of three office girls who're lambasting me. This gives them a fright. That's it, I think. I am a Rightist. I'm seized by a sudden, intense joy. It makes me shiver. I've touched the essence of myself. I am a Rightist!

I move a step closer to the girls. They hold each other and raise faint, frightened cries of protest. I place myself in front of the girls and the men standing nearby.

Without speaking a word, I face the whole lot, my eyes filled with hostility and hate. They all stare at me. I am a Rightist! Even though they're staring at me, I'm not flustered. I don't blush. I feel a new me. These others no longer see the wretched me who wets his penis in masturbation, giving it the moist look of a green stem of grass that's just been snapped off. They no longer see the lonely, miserable, timid Seventeen. They don't look at me with the threatening eyes of those others who, after just one glance, say, "We can see right through you."

Adults now look at me the way they look at other adults who possess an independent personality. I feel like I've wrapped my weak, petty self inside strong armor, forever to be hidden from the eyes of others. It's the armor of the Right. When I move another step closer to the girls, they scream. But they don't manage to escape. It's like their legs are paralyzed. Hot blood is visibly pulsing in the girls' chests. Their fear arouses in me an intense spiritual joy akin to sexual desire. I scream out at them.

"What about the Rightists, then? What about us Rightists, you bitches?"

Instead of screaming, they at last decide to run away into the crowded twilight streets. The remaining men grumble out their discontent, trying at the same time to hide the fact that they're afraid of me. So. The Others are afraid of me.

The men are finally determined to take care of the scandal I showered them with, like so much confetti, by using the word *bitches*. But just then people wearing armbands that say Imperial Way gather around me. Together we are the Right.

A strong hand, a friendly, passionate, sinewy hand plants itself firmly on my shoulder. I turn to see an elderly man in an exaltation of intense passion. I'm fascinated by his big, bloodshot, burning eyes. Like a child filled with admiration, I smile at this preacher of malice and hate.

"Thank you," he says. "I've been waiting for a pure and brave patriotic youngster like you. You are the son of Japan who can fulfill the Heart of His Majesty the Emperor. It is you, the chosen boy with the true Japanese soul."

The voice of revelation gains ascendancy over the din and bustle, over the trains, the speakers, and all the howling voices of the metropolis. It reaches out to me, beautiful and gentle as a rose. Again I'm captured by a hysterical hallucination. The city at dusk sinks away into the darkness. It carries a glitter within, like ink mingled with dark gold paint. Brilliantly, the rising sun appears from it. It is a golden being, it is a god, I feel it. It is the Emperor.

"You are the son of Japan who can fulfill the Heart of His Majesty the Emperor. It is you, the Chosen Boy with the true Japanese soul!"

4

At the Headquarters of the Imperial Way, I'm sworn in as a member of the Party. Later, Kunihiko Sakakibara announces that I'm the youngest member in the history of the group. This leads me to believe that I won't find any other teenagers at the Headquarters when I move in, but actually I discover three nineteen-year-old members. These guys, however, couldn't be further from my image of teenagers. These teens of the Right are proud and solemn. They never drop their stern, grave expressions. When I mention something like movies, jazz, or popular music, they lash out in contempt. They accuse me of being a frivolous brat. Whenever they use that kind of language, I line up small round lumps of mud, one by one, at the edge of my anthole of the Right, as tokens of my despair.

These young Rightists are the spitting image of the car-

icature I'd formed in my irresponsible daydreams, before I
joined the party. Even in their deadly seriousness they
resemble that image to the tee. I remember once seeing an ad
for a film called *The Emperor Meiji and the Great Russo-
Japanese War*. I thought that was probably the kind of
movie young right-wingers would go to see. When I ask
them about it, for the first time they get really wrapped up
in the subject of the film. They tell me they adore it, and
have seen it several times. Then they get into an animated
discussion among themselves, like the film had broken every
record in cinema history. In the process, they completely
confuse the actors and the historical people, making solemn
statements like "His Majesty the Emperor Meiji gazed at
His troops with a sorrowful look," or "General Nogi's
horse was tremendous. Admiral Togo didn't show a hint of
exhaustion on his face, not even on the battlefield—the true
warrior spirit. A warrior has to take care of his health and be
in perfect condition in time of need." Apparently they also
go to the theater occasionally if there's a war movie on, or
some historical sword-fighting movie. In the war movies,
some of the scenes that show Japanese soldiers in action are
enough to make their hearts leap. And the sword-play
movies show the techniques for killing with the sword.
They treat Westerns and modern gangster movies with contempt and disdain, since pistols are used in movies like that.
They can't get their hands on pistols, and anyway, the boss
wouldn't allow it. After all, it's only natural that the technique for committing the perfect murder with a Japanese

sword is more valuable to them, and more real. One of the teenagers in particular has a cherished picture of the naked human body, to which he's added red spots, as if they were the points for applying acupuncture needles. One morning, when somebody is stabbed to death in an incident in Shinjuku, I understand what those red marks really mean. I notice how the teenager explores the newspaper, and then adds new red marks to certain parts of the body. With a still-fresh curiosity about my new companions, I ask him, "Are you planning to stab somebody too?"

He sternly closes his eyes, as if offering a silent prayer, and in a fierce, solitary voice that doesn't seem to be directed at me, he says, "If those bastards don't cut out the funny business, if the Leftists keep on with their funny business, I will."

My companion frets over the words *funny business*. He knits his brow as he racks his brains for some more appropriate expression. But I think I understand his feelings. That's right: "If those bastards don't cut out their funny business." That's all that needs to be said between members of the Imperial Way. There's no need for further elaboration. For sure, young members of the Imperial Way don't have glib tongues. The boss is an eloquent orator, and some of the executives are just as good, but the young faction members are definitely not talkers. They aren't even talkative in everyday life. Mostly they tend to hold their tongues. When the time comes for speeches, we scream and shout like the enemy is standing there in front of our very eyes with his weapon drawn. We glare and shake our fists. "We have to stop those Reds from doing any funny business!"

Occasionally we members of the Imperial Way get together with nonmembers like the youth department of the Conservative party. We keep our mouths shut tight and put up with the gabble of their young men, who, unlike us, devote all their energy to talk. Deep down, the young members of the Imperial Way despise the young men of the Conservative party. At members-only meetings of the Imperial Way, we accuse them of being time-servers. "Those bastards don't think about anything but their careers. Just talk and more talk, trying to get themselves ahead. They're no different from the careerists of the Left. They ought to stop their funny business too . . ."

I recall a postcard I got once from some provincial member of the youth department of the Conservative party. Although he only knew me by sight, the dirty red-cheeked yakker confided every detail of his future plans to me.

"I've put 200,000 in the stock market," he wrote, "and my stocks are growing steadily. At this moment I'm twenty-four. My ambition is to be in the City Assembly at twenty-five, to be a Dietman at thirty, and a Cabinet member at thirty-five. I'm aiming at financial power through stocks on the one hand, and on the other, at participation in a Party faction as Head of the Publicity Department of the Party Youth Section of the Bunkyo Ward Office. I believe in the principle of promotion through personal merit, so whenever I go to the Party Headquarters I challenge the Party executive to discussions on equal terms. The other day, at a certain restaurant in town, I debated for two hours with the Secretary-General of the Party about global and national situations. I really threw the dust in his eyes. When I'm named to the Cabinet, I suppose that you, brother, will have grown into a man of influence in the nonparliamentary groups. This thought fills me with joy, and so I have decided to begin this correspondence. Let us exchange opinions extensively. Please allow me also to introduce you to the President of Matsukawa Securities for stock matters, and for political matters, to Mr. Kikuyama, Head of the Information and Publicity Department."

I was shocked and astonished by this. Guys like him are really jaundiced country bumpkins, wanting only to cling to their own careers. Sometimes, young members of the Imperial Way clash with people like him. They thrash us with words, but we answer by glaring back at them in threatening silence, and it soon becomes obvious that we're in the right. It never does us any good to associate with these garrulous creatures. We learn only from our boss. We only read things he recommends to us. That's how we gather the wisdom that sustains us. It's not a lot of wisdom, mind you, it's only a tiny bit of golden wisdom which, as a solid belief, is hammered deep into our heads like a hard, hot nail. And it turns us into hard, hot nails as well. This applies to me in particular. Since the evening in late spring when I had that decisive change of heart, I learn only from the voice of the boss, and read only the things he provides to me. Pure and simple, only that.

SEVENTEEN

Everything else I reject with hatred and hostility.

I'm convinced that Kunihiko Sakakibara gives me preferential treatment. And I think I respond sufficiently to the passion he pours into me. This is how he puts it: "The way we pound our ideology into you is like pouring sake into a ready bottle. Your bottle doesn't break as we pour. This pure, beautiful wine doesn't spill. You are the chosen young man, and the Right is a chosen existence. By now this must be as clear as the sun, even to the blind of this world. Such is Justice."

A few weeks pass since that night, and Kunihiko Sakakibara visits our house to receive my parents' blessing for his intention to have me move into the Imperial Way Headquarters. Father, with his typical American liberal attitude, says he doesn't intend to interfere with me in finding my own way, as long as I don't cause any trouble for the family. He adds some flattering remarks to Sakakibara, saying that if I have to get involved in a political movement, at least one based on patriotism is sounder than the Red Student Coalition. I recall how my father once said, contrary to his American liberalism, that his position as a teacher would be compromised if his son got involved in the student movement. So I think I'm on safe ground with the old man.

When I look at my brother, he turns away, like he's bewildered. My mother, like the time I hurt my sister, doesn't say anything to my face. When Sakakibara praises my sister for her work as an SDF nurse, she answers that a lot of her fellow nurses have read his book, *The Way to Truly Love Japan and the Japanese*. Her voice is so faint it seems to be coming from an earphone, and her blush is so red it's almost vulgar. Then Sakakibara thanks the whole family for accepting my move into the Headquarters, vows lifelong responsibility for me, and bids his farewell. I'm left with the family, who immediately want to know when I joined a rightist group and got to know such important people. I silence them all with a lie. "After sis went to work as an SDF nurse, I couldn't stomach people bad-mouthing the SDF." I realize I've gained the power to beat back my whole family with one good blow. Only five weeks have passed since the day of my seventeenth birthday, when my sister argued me down and made me cry. But a miracle has happened. I've become a different person. I am transformed.

My transformation has its most dramatic effect at school. Now that I've officially joined the Imperial Way, the big-talking Shintoho knows that I've found him out. He was never anything but an emotional sympathizer of the Party. Since then, he's functioned as my publicity agent and biographer. According to Shintoho, I've been a rightist for years. My fiasco in the eight-hundred-meter race, which was such a humiliating experience to me, he turns into "a rightist expression of contempt for the coach."

"This guy, you understand, on the square at Shinbashi Station, this guy single-handedly took on no less than twenty Commies who'd come to abuse the Right. Kunihiko Sakakibara considers him his personal successor. That's why he's at the Imperial Way Headquarters all the time. He's a true, born Rightist."

Before long, everybody in the school knows I'm a Rightist and a member of the Imperial Way. It turns into a major scandal in the staff room. When one of the teachers dresses me down about it, I tell him that if they're going to tolerate left-wing students, then rightist shouldn't be any problem. When a teacher breathes so much as a word of criticism about the Right, I ask him in a roundabout way if he'd mind my passing his comment on to Kunihiko Sakakibara. In more indirect terms, I hint at the influence of the Imperial Way. The teachers are even more deeply affected by Shintoho's demagoguery than the students, so my hints are more than sufficient. Rumor has it that the world history teacher turns ultraconservative only when I attend class. It's not that there aren't people who show hostility to me for being a rightist. The members of the student council, who are scheming to link up with the student union and join in demonstrations, start arguments with me. But I always win simply by turning the doubts I used to feel about the ideas of the left-wing leaders on their head. The same way my sister trounced me on the night of my birthday, I trounce them now. They don't have confidence in their own firm grasp of ideas about peace, about rearmament, about the Soviet Union and China, about America. All I have to do is attack their weaknesses. And I always hold a trump. "Most of the intellectuals in Japan are left-wing these days. The Right is in the minority. But I'd rather side with the farmers' sons who join the SDF because they didn't want to starve than with a progressive clique of big-shot university professors. Professors are honorable enough, and believe in principle, but is that enough? If your beloved professors rush to the UN to make an appeal, maybe they'll stop some local war in the Far East. But I want to stand by those poor Japanese farm boys who're getting killed in the meantime, in a matter of days, by the army of Syngman Rhee. Anyway, none other than your favorite hero Sartre says 'What's the point in talking about justice if you don't intend to put it into practice?' I may only be a weak, stupid human being, but I'm willing to risk my life for the Youth Movement of the Right. Is there one single one of you who's joined the Communist Party, and is selflessly devoting himself to it? Aren't you all planning to go on to Tokyo University, and eventually be executives in some big company?"

I recall how once, from behind these pale, dumbstruck geniuses, the proud Emiko Sugi looked at me with excited eyes that clearly showed her interest in me. "Old-fashioned right-wing boys like you," she said, "go all the way to the Military Academy, don't they?"

I told Kunihiko Sakakibara that I wanted to enter the Military Academy, gather a group around me, and eventually gain enough power to carry off a coup. Sakakibara responded to my ambition with an obvious look of deep gratification that warmed me with an intense feeling of joy.

The uniform of the Imperial Way is modeled on the Nazi SS uniform. It gives me strength when I walk the streets, and an intense, memorable joy. I feel like I've gone to heaven, and my body is covered with an unyielding armor, like the carapace of a beetle. The tender, weak, vulnerable, unshapely creature inside is invisible to others. When people looked at me before, I'd blush in fright. I was captured by a·timorous, miserable self-loathing. I was bound hand and foot by self-consciousness. But now, instead of seeing what's inside me, others see the uniform of the Right. More than that, it instills them with fear. Behind the impenetrable curtain of the right-wing uniform I can hide forever the soul of an easily wounded young man. I am no longer ashamed, no longer hurt by the eyes of others. And gradually this sensation grows, to the point where, even when I don't wear the uniform, even when I'm naked, the eyes of others have lost the power to hurt me with shame.

I used to think that if I ever got caught masturbating, I'd kill myself in shame. It was a tragic drama between the overwhelming power of the eyes of others, and the utter weakness of my own flesh, ashamed and afraid. But one day I have a decisive experience. It makes the crisis itself of this drama meaningless, and reduces it to dust.

It all starts with an exchange between Kunihiko Sakakibara and me.

"You must be bothered by sexual needs sometimes," he says. "It's useless to suppress them. Do you want to sleep with a woman?"

"No, I don't think so."

"Well, then. Let's do this. You have a woman at the

Turkish bath give your manhood a rub. Take this money and go."

At first I can't imagine it. I don't believe my shame has really been rooted out. A fellow member tells me to go in uniform. The code of ethics says that the official uniform of the Imperial Way can only be worn in daytime. It's night, but I feel shaky, so I follow his advice.

Clad in the armor of the Right, I enter through the decorated glass doors of a Turkish bath in the old red-light district of Shinjuku. Instead of having an erection, I'm pale and dizzy, like a pitiful child about to receive a terrible punishment. For the first time since I joined the Party, I resent the boss. But then the uniform of the Imperial Way becomes a sustaining weight, heavier than a lead diving suit. In the instant that follows, I know that for those others, the armor of the Right is something that sends up fear more violently than a leather straightjacket.

The girl's face is pale and straw-colored, but she has a nice figure. Wearing nothing but a white bra and short pants, she welcomes me into a pink-walled room. For exactly five seconds, no more, she looks at my uniform in the glow of the bare, steam-wet lightbulb. Her face cringes, and she averts her eyes. She doesn't lift them again. For the first time in my life I become undressed before the eyes of another. What's more, I'm naked before the eyes of a young girl. At long last I feel that my brittle, naked body with its budding muscles is covered with a coat of mail, thick as the walls of an armored car. It's the armor of the Right. I have an enormous erection. It is I, a man with his manhood (*manhood* is what Kunihiko Sakakibara called it) like a red-hot skewer ready to pierce through the virgin vagina of a newly wed bride. I will keep this erection through my entire life. It is precisely the miracle I had wished for on my seventeenth birthday, when I was smeared with pitiful tears. All my life will be an orgasm. My body, my soul, all of me will continue to stand erect.

In the jungles of South America there's a tribe where the men always have an erection. The gods, worried that the sex of these men would be a hindrance to hunting and warfare, attached them to their bellies, like the sex of dogs. I am a Seventeen of their tribe.

The girl guides me into the steam bath, washes and rinses me, puts me into the bathtub, rubs me dry with a towel, sprinkles powder over me, and has me lie down on what looks like the bed in a doctor's office. During the massage, she starts to caress my manhood, gently and in silence. As quietly as if she were praying to a god, she peels back my foreskin, which is deformed from my masturbation habit. Her fingertips are apprehensive and afraid.

I lie on my back, proud as a king. The girl is blushing with shame, like she's performing a vicious, embarrassing act. I'm reminded of a verse from a poem in one of my sister's poetry books. I copied it in one of my letters to Emiko Sugi, although eventually I tore it up.

> Stand on the highest pavement of the stairs—
> Lean on a garden urn—

Kenzaburo Oe

Weave, weave the sunlight in your hair—
Clasp your flowers to you with pained surprise—

My manhood is the sunlight. My manhood is a flower.
I'm seized by the pleasant sensation of an intense orgasm.
Again I see the golden being floating in the dark sky. I cry
with pleasure. His Majesty the Emperor! His Majesty the
Emperor, the radiant sun . . .

When I finally recover from this hysterical hallucination, I see my semen spattered on the girl's cheeks like glistening tears. Instead of feeling the usual postmasturbation
depression, I'm lost in a triumphant joy. I don't say a word
to this female slave as I put on my Imperial Way uniform.
That's the correct attitude.

Tonight I've learned three lessons: I, the rightist young
man, have completely conquered the eyes of others; I, the
rightist young man, have the right to commit any atrocity
on the weak others; and I, the rightist young man, am a child
of His Majesty the Emperor.

I am driven by a passionate desire to learn more about
His Majesty. Until now, I had always thought that the only
people who have any relationship with the Emperor are
those who were determined to die for him during the war,
like my brother's and older generations. Whenever I heard
people from the war generation talk about the Emperor, I
felt jealousy and antipathy. But that was wrong. For I am a
child of the Right. I am a child of His Majesty the Emperor.

I start to spend a lot of time in Kunihiko Sakakibara's

library, looking for books that will tell me what I want to know about the Emperor. I read the *Records of Ancient Matters, Anthology of Poems by the Emperor Meiji*, and the books used to educate my predecessors of the Divine Soldiers and the Institute of the Great East. I read *Mein Kampf*. And at the suggestion of Kunihiko Sakakibara, I read Masaharu Taniguchi's *Imperial Absolutism and Its Influence*. I'm beside myself with gratitude, since this book gives me what I've been yearning for. I cling to its essential principle: "Devotion and selfishness are incompatible."

That's right, I think, my passion ablaze. Devotion and selfishness are incompatible. I was a prisoner of impotence because of my selfishness, and couldn't grasp the real world, trembling as I was with anxiety and the fear of death. My selfish ego made me feel weird, filled with conflict and swollen with incoherence, confusion, and obscenity. The anxiety was unbearable. Every time I did anything, I wondered if I hadn't made the wrong choice. Anxiety, always anxiety. It was unbearable. But devotion is incompatible with selfishness. That's right. I'll throw away my selfishness, and offer my spirit and body entirely to His Majesty the Emperor.

Cast away selfishness, and forsake myself completely!

I feel the fog of gnawing contradictions that I've known until now being burned away. The fog that robbed me of my self-confidence is now blown away, and with it the mass of unresolved contradictions. The fog is swept away. His Majesty the Emperor has ordered me to cast away the fog of selfishness, and I have cast it away. The individual I is dead. Selfishness is dead. The instant I slaughtered my selfishness, the instant I locked the individual I into the dungeon, a new I was born, a child of the Emperor without anxiety. I feel liberated. I no longer know the anxiety of those who have to choose. His Majesty the Emperor makes the choices. Stones and trees don't know anxiety, they can't fall into uncertainty. By casting away my selfishness, I have become a stone, a tree of His Majesty the Emperor. I have no anxiety, I cannot fall into uncertainty. I feel that I can go on living without burden. I feel I can give a plain and simple interpretation of a real world that once was so complicated and incomprehensible. It is the truth that devotion and selfishness are incompatible.

The blessed reward of the man who has cast away his selfishness is devotion! I realize that in only an instant I've lost my fear of death. Death, which once made me tremble desperately with fear, now seems completely meaningless. The fear cannot be summoned or aroused again. Even if I die, I will not perish. I am only one young leaf on the giant tree of eternity, which is His Majesty the Emperor. I will never perish! My fear of death is conquered. Emperor, You are my God, my Sun, my Eternity. Through You I have truly started to live!

I have reached my goal, and leave Kunihiko Sakakibara's library. I have no further need of books. I start to dedicate myself to karate and judo. On my training clothes Sakakibara kindly writes, "Seven lives in service of the country, long live His Majesty the Emperor."

I believe the time is now right for me to cry out to myself the words Sakakibara once spoke to me: "It is you, the Chosen Boy with the true Japanese soul!"

May. The leftists have started organizing regular marches on the Diet. I eagerly join the Youth Group of the Imperial Way. Red workers, red students, red artists, red actors—beat them, kick them, pursue them!

The steel code of ethics of our Youth Group is based on the speech the Nazi Himmler delivered, roaring like a lion, at a congress of SS officers at Poznan on the fourth of April, 1943.

One, loyalty; two, obedience; three, courage; four, sincerity; five, honesty; six, comradeship; seven, responsible joy; eight, diligence; nine, abstinence from alcohol; ten, what we view as important and consider our duty is our Emperor and our patriotism: There is no need for us to heed anything else.

Trample the Reds, knock them down, stab them to death, strangle them, burn them!

I fight like a hero. I wield my stick of malice at the students, I swing my nail-studded wooden sword of hostility into a group of women. I trample them, I pursue them.

Time after time I'm arrested, but as soon as I'm released, I take up my attacks on the demonstrating mob. Again I'm arrested, again I'm released.

Twenty members of the Youth Group of the Imperial Way stand against ten thousand leftists. I am the most heroic, the most ferocious of them all. I am the Seventeen, more

Right than any other. Rampaging through the riots, deep into the night, I'm the one and only blissful Seventeen who sees the radiant Emperor appearing with a golden halo from the darkness of this gloomy, intense night of insults, screams, and cries of pain and fear.

A drizzling rain is falling in the night. The rumor that a female student has died instantly returns the confused crowd to stillness. When the weeping students hold a silent prayer, drenched by the rain and crushed by discomfort, sadness, and pain, I experience the orgasm of a rapist. To my golden vision I promise a bloodbath. I am the one and only blissful Seventeen.

J

Part One

THE BIG IVORY JAGUAR came rushing headlong through the darkness to the edge of the cape's ridge. Facing the night sea, it turned right and disappeared down a side road that dropped with the sudden steepness of a waterfall. The Jaguar was headed toward Miminashi Bay, which was hidden like an armpit under the south side of the cape. A 16-millimeter Arriflex movie camera was packed in the car. The camera, like the car, was the property of a young man of twenty-nine whom everybody called J. J, his wife, J's sister (who was driving), a middle-aged cameraman, a young poet, a twenty-year-old actor, and an eighteen-year-old jazz singer—seven in all—were on their way to J's vacation house. They were going there to shoot a few scenes for a short film J's wife was making.

The jazz singer was completely naked. She was singing a drunken song. Since nobody was listening with very much interest she was convinced that everybody in the Jaguar was mocking her, so she decided to try a dirty story she'd had some success with once before. For the four hours that they'd been on the way from Tokyo everybody (with the exception of J's sister) had been steadily drinking whisky. The eighteen-year-old singer had been the first to break from the ranks of the drunks and now was running alone in the lead. This was what always happened. She lacked self-restraint.

"Once when I went to do a job at this politician's party," she said, "there was this sixteen-year-old girl who was with me in the dressing room, without any makeup on, and she was sitting there with this Ping-Pong ball and a blue vinyl costume across her knees. So we became friends. When it was her turn to go on the girl still hadn't put on any make-up. She just took off her clothes. She pulled her costume, which looked like a blue vinyl sleeping bag, over her head, and she had me pull the zipper to the lower part of her back. The blue dress was really a frog costume that hugged her body, with a hole that looked like a fish mouth between her legs. The politicians all looked at this blue frog with a girl's privates, and then she put the Ping-Pong ball inside herself. And, if you can believe it, she croaked like a frog in time to her dancing!"

The other six passengers raised their voices in a dispirited laugh. They all knew that if they didn't respond, the singer would start crying and fly into a rage.

Cheered by their laughter, the singer went on.

"That frog dancer had marvellous technique," she said

with a look of triumph, as though she was building to some climax. "Truly marvellous technique."

"Your politicians weren't looking at technique, they wanted to see how shameless a sixteen-year-old could be," J said. He was sitting between his wife and his sister in the front seat. "That's the one thing that never changes, no matter what kind of dirty act you put on. The spectators don't want a display of technique that makes your embarrassment obvious. Shamelessness is what they want to see. They want to see it in the flesh!"

The eighteen-year-old jazz singer gave up. Her mood turned black and she started to sob. Everybody, including J's wife, knew that J and the singer were having an affair. The eighteen-year-old girl looked more and more disconsolate. Her naked shoulders shook as she cried. If they hadn't been in the car she'd probably have reached for a knife or a broken bottle and lashed out like a panic-stricken cat.

"Why do you have to be so nasty?" J's sister complained. "Besides, it's dark and this road isn't exactly straight. So maybe you could do us a favor and quiet down just a little bit? Or do you want to die before we get there, without finishing that film of yours?" She couldn't stand her older brother's meanness, with its strange psychological twists.

Except for J's sister and the crying girl, everyone else was smiling in silence, drinking, and listening to the sound of the engine and the sounds inside themselves. They didn't ask themselves why they were smiling. Whenever there was

J

a silence they smiled this kind of magnanimous smile.

The Jaguar had reached the bottom of the hill at the right side of the bay. Turning to the left, it passed slowly over the narrow flagstone road through Miminashi Village.

"Could you please close the window?" J's sister said. "I hate the smell of dead fish and nets. You don't mind, do you?"

Two of the others closed the windows.

Then J's sister turned to J. "It doesn't matter how carefully I drive. You're still going to find some scratches in the morning," she said with what sounded like regret. "Why don't you drive? You're the genius at the wheel."

"Too dangerous when I'm drunk," J replied, still smiling and barely moving his lips. "We'd end up in the bay."

The car moved along the stone roadway, occasionally passing over channels brimming with seawater. The road curved gently, hugging the inside of the bay as it joined one village with the next. Houses lined the sides of the road, looking like rows of dead elephants. Clusters of dark gray houses turned in on themselves giving the impression of being completely closed up. A lamp threw a faint light from the direction of the sea beyond the channels. There was a beacon of a fishing boat at anchor. The cluster of houses was in shadow.

The Jaguar moved slowly ahead with a sound even quieter than the calm sea. Suddenly the headlights caught a group of people on the stone pavement ahead, and J's sister stepped on the brakes. The whisky bottles clattered as they

fell from the seat. The eighteen-year-old singer stopped crying and was about to scold, but she decided to keep silent.
Everybody in the car was curious and stared at the people in
the headlights.

In the sudden powerful light about thirty fisher folk
shrank back like blind mice. Most were women, but among
them were a few old people and children. The women were
all wearing deep-colored, thick-woven clothing in the Ainu
style. All seemed to be about the same age, with the same
middle-aged look. An assembly of middle-aged women, in a
bad mood and possessed by some fervor. The headlights
made their faces appear ugly, animal-like, and petty. They
were waiting in front of one house, completely blocking the
road. Now all the faces were turned toward the Jaguar, but
they gave the distinct feeling that only an instant before they
had all been staring at the house.

"Hide Keiko," J's sister said. "Put her down on the
floor and put a jacket over her head!"

Keiko Sawa was the jazz singer's name. She did as she
was told. Her small naked girl's body, kneeling with her side
and hips pressed against the back of the front seat, was covered with a jacket and a skirt and some other things. The
other three in the back seat held her with their knees so she
wouldn't fall when the car started to move again. The Jaguar
inched toward the crowd. J hesitantly reached out for the
horn, but his sister stopped him. "Don't!" she said, frightened but still stern. "If you do that they'll turn over the car
and burn it. They're starting to move over on their own."

J

And, sure enough, as the Jaguar approached, the crowd flowed back quietly under the eaves of the houses lining the stone road. It seemed as if they'd already lost interest in the car and the seven people in it. In fact, they appeared to be totally indifferent. Those in the car wanted to feel the same, but the naked crouching girl was shaking. When the car started to pass through the crowd, they realized for the first time that the house on the seaward side of the village that everyone had been watching was the only one where a light was burning, behind an open window on the second floor, and that that light had illuminated the flagstone road and the faces of those people.

As the Jaguar passed it began to pick up speed. At first they all were depressed and silent. They felt as though they'd been intimidated. Then the middle-aged cameraman, who always broke the tension at times like these, gave a hearty laugh. (When he laughed, it was always a hearty one.) "Weren't we just like a team of explorers going through some native village?" he said. "If we don't do something to stir them up they won't do anything. It reminded me of when I was in Borneo to make an educational film! It also reminded me of a Western."

Keiko Sawa raised her naked body and sat down on the cameraman's short, fat legs. "Were they Indians?" she asked in a wheedling voice that was subdued and more sober than before.

"Those people live in the village," J's sister said. "The men are out fishing, so it's everybody who's left, don't you think? I've done clay heads of some of the people who live around the bay." She was a twenty-seven-year-old sculptor and had come back from Paris at the beginning of the summer. She was probably doing the artwork for the film J and his wife were making.

"Shouldn't we have stopped the car and asked for fish for tomorrow?" J said critically.

"You don't know anything at all about the villages around this bay. When we were evacuated here during the war, you were so afraid to come down to the bay that you stayed in the house all day long drawing pictures! You were scared of the fishermen's kids!"

The Jaguar followed the flagstone road to the end of the village, then took a slight detour that allowed the seven to look down at the bile-black sea on the far side of a low breakwater. Then the Jaguar started to climb again. The branches of the scrub trees, defeated by the sea breeze, reached out to the windshield in the tortured shapes of arms wrenched around by violence. The sound of the branches beating the Jaguar made the seven passengers feel for an instant as if they were trapped in a squall.

"I wasn't scared of the fishermen's children. But I resented the fact that the people in the bay were afraid of our family just because we had land and a cabin in the mountains. That's why I didn't go down there. I wasn't as insensitive as you," J said.

"Those startled faces, so full of resentment," Keiko Sawa said. "Didn't they look just like people caught by a stranger in the middle of having sex?"

Everybody but J's sister laughed at that.

"You probably wouldn't even mind if somebody caught you having sex, would you, Keiko?" the cameraman said. "Still, your powers of observation are sometimes quite strong."

"Those people were there to shame a woman for adultery," J's sister said in a low, gloomy voice, as if she were whispering something to her brother alone. "The same thing happened when we were evacuated here. The adulterous woman is hiding in the house. We couldn't see it because of the people, but I think the doors in and out of the house were boarded shut."

"What were they doing, gathering there in the middle of the night? What do you mean when you say 'shame her'?"

"They just stand there in front of the house, all the women and old people and children in the village. Even the men when they're not fishing! Isn't that enough to shame somebody? It makes me sick, just thinking about it."

"It does; it makes me sick too," the twenty-year-old actor said from the back seat. "It's disgusting, for something like adultery."

"Of course it'd make you sick, Boy. People all over Tokyo would be showing up in front of your apartment every night!" the cameraman said, referring to the actor.

"Really—thanks to Boy, at least a hundred husbands know what adultery is now," the naked jazz singer said, treating the actor like he was less than her equal in age.

The Jaguar climbed the road that zigzagged up the slope until it came out on the high ground that enclosed the bay and suddenly looked down on the village.

"Say, stop the car," the cameraman said. "Wasn't there a light in the second-floor window of the house those people were standing around? Maybe we can see something."

The seven got out of the Jaguar. Keiko Sawa took the blanket that had been spread out on the seat and wrapped it around her shoulders like a Mexican poncho. The cameraman connected some photographic lenses to make a telescope. He worked for a company that made educational and promotional films, but he was an outsider in the company, an old-fashioned type who wasn't interested in appearances and didn't dance to the same tune as his colleagues. When it had become clear that he wasn't going to be accepted by the company or get ahead, he grew a beard, traded his gray suit for a stained sweater, and started driving an old-fashioned car. He put all his energy into elaborate inventions. Assembling telescopic lenses was just one of his hobbies. And when he heard that his young friends were going to make a movie, he put his family and his company work on hold, giving himself to this precarious job. He was a terribly frustrated man in his forties. It couldn't be said that he had any great talent, but he really was a good person; he was a drinker, but not lazy. Even if he could no longer stir up any interest in his work for the company that didn't mean he neglected it. Tomorrow, after the one-hour shoot at daybreak he'd probably drive back to Tokyo alone to put in some hours there.

When he finished adjusting the telescope, the seven took turns peeping into the only lighted window in the village below. They could see a woman bending over and busily moving her arms, but what she was doing wasn't exactly clear. The seven continued to look for a long time, but the movements of the woman's body didn't change. From where they were they could see only the woman's back and the shaking of her rich, tangled hair. What she was doing with her arms was obscure. Still, the violent up-and-down movement of her shoulders was deeply impressive. They watched for a long time, until finally they grew tired of it— or rather, until they grew tired of their own unsatisfied curiosity.

"Let's go back to the car," Keiko said. "I'm cold." She had picked the right moment. This eighteen-year-old nymphomaniac had that kind of sense about her, a keenness that you'd expect to find only in the antennae of a beetle.

With that, they all gave up trying to figure out the meaning of the woman's movements and went back to the Jaguar. J, his wife, and his sister sat in front, while the cameraman, the jazz singer, the actor, and the young poet, who'd been silently drinking whisky all along, sat in back. The Jaguar got going.

The young poet was twenty-five years old. He had published only one volume of poems, and that at his own expense. As a friend of J's young wife, he had taken on the job of providing commentary for the movie. He had been her college classmate. In their final year, they had been extremely close. They'd also slept together more than once. In those days, J's wife, poor as she was, had been like a proud lioness, with her heart set on becoming a film director. When they graduated he and his film-obsessed classmate had gone different ways, but a year later a wedding invitation had reached him. His classmate's husband, J, was the son of a steel company president and four years older than the two of them. It was J's hobby to be a patron of the arts. He had a 16-millimeter movie camera, an artist for a sister, an ivory Jaguar with white tires and spoked wheels, a vacation house that looked out over a bay—and even a round-the-world ticket on Pan American. He'd also picked his father's pockets so that his wife could make a movie. The young poet's classmate was crazy about J, and she was crazy about her film project. The poet had used his friendship with her to borrow money from J, to publish his collection of poems. In exchange, he'd agreed to write the commentary for the film. He'd become a friend of the new couple, but he had never managed to conquer a distinct feeling of distance where J was concerned. Was he jealous of the husband of a classmate he'd slept with in the past? His classmate invited him to parties J gave at their gorgeous apartment, where he was collecting young actors and singers. Was that only her idea, or had J wanted it too? He didn't know the answer to that question and it left him insecure.

"Well, what do you make of it?" J said to his wife. Like

J

the young poet, she had been silent all night. She was drinking whisky straight from the bottle.

"The woman was washing rice," his wife said without thinking.

That's it, they all felt. That woman, who had been hunted down for adultery, was patiently enduring, even resisting, while washing rice. All seven were silent, lost in their own thoughts about the woman who was washing rice in spite of the intimidation and about the angry people who had planted themselves in front of her house. Finally, the twenty-year-old actor spoke.

"Why was the window open?"

At first nobody answered. He felt injured by their silence and blushed. The poet noticed.

"Because it's hot, I suppose. It's cooler now, because it's the middle of the night, but she's probably been washing rice since sundown, when it was still hot indoors if you were moving around."

"Today was the hottest day this summer. But why wouldn't she close the window now, when it's after dark and cooler?"

"She's probably afraid of provoking the crowd outside."

"It makes me sick," the actor said.

They were all silent again. Some of them shivered. In low gear, the Jaguar climbed to the top of the ridge on the south side of the bay.

~

When they reached the mountain house, the seven unloaded the camera equipment, whisky and gin bottles, food, portable recorder and tapes, several books and notebooks, and some other things from the Jaguar. Since it was chilly, the jazz singer put on her underwear, bending her neck and back double in the cramped space inside the car; but it was too difficult to put on clothes, and finally she got out with a one-piece satin dress and a checkered blanket clasped to her sides. Everybody, including the singer, had sobered up by now. So they all wanted a drink.

The mountain villa was supported by log pillars and steel cable and projected like a fisherman's basket from a narrow space of flat land that had been carved out of the slope facing the bay. The Jaguar was parked directly under the house. To get to the house, they climbed a steep ladder that was hung from the cliff, and when all seven had climbed the ladder, the ivory Jaguar was already lost in the thick darkness. Dark sky, black clouds. The village and the sea spread out beneath them, as black as the clouds.

When they'd gone inside and turned on the lights the seven felt a little less threatened. On the side away from the sea the house opened onto a broad garden, which was joined to a balcony only slightly lower than the first floor of the villa and gradually became higher and more open. So, even looking down from the second-floor windows the garden didn't seem particularly low. The lights in the main hall made the lush summer grass that grew at the edge of the balcony float up in vivid greens. The garden in darkness was a

J

color reminiscent of black printed on the blue ground of a lithograph. The seven put their luggage down in the hall and stared through a wide glass door at the darkness of the garden.

"The first floor is only this one main room, although there is a bathroom and toilet, and the kitchen in the back. Upstairs we have three bedrooms and closets. The rooms are all separate, like in a hotel, so anybody who wants to be by himself can use them. But it's going to be cold." The twenty-seven-year-old sculptor made this explanation to the four guests who were visiting the vacation house for the first time, and not to her brother and his wife.

"It's really cold, even if it is August!" said the cameraman. "It's enough to scare off even the farmers from the Northeast. I spent some time up there once to get footage of the frost damage, but they scare as quick as a bunch of poor dogs. I'm catching a cold, J!" The cameraman shivered as he spoke, and his cheeks, discolored by drinking, had turned the color of grapes.

The first person to call this young man "J" had been his sister's foreign teacher, probably because J's father had given him a long, pompous name that was too hard for foreigners to remember. After that, everybody, including J himself, had started to call him "J." The ambiguous impression of being a fictional character with the initial J for a name suited him perfectly.

"You're one of those people who can't stand the cold, aren't you? Is it really true that you went to the South Pole on a whaler taking pictures? I'm surprised you didn't freeze to death."

"It's true. But hating the cold has nothing to do with freezing to death, Keiko. You're so sure you can stand the cold, you run around naked all the time. You'll freeze to death before you know it. Of course, sometimes we'd have camera trouble at the South Pole, and I'd be out there like a repairman."

J's sister and wife brought some kindling and newspapers from the kitchen and put them into the fireplace; but as soon as they tried to start a fire, the cameraman took the job on himself.

"I've got a technique for starting fires. I wouldn't need matches to set a house on fire," he said, but his obvious pride had a hollow ring.

The rest, except for the lazy J, brought chairs from the other part of the room and arranged them in a circle around the fireplace. Then they pushed the sofa and table into a corner away from the fireplace because somebody might want to dance. And, since they'd taken the trouble to turn the sofa to the wall, it would also be possible to sleep in the room without being bothered.

Smoke and odors filled the room. The middle-aged cameraman got up from the fire. His cheeks had lost their purplish color; the sake red had returned. The smoke had gotten to him, and one teardrop trickled down each of his cheeks as far as the edge of his lips; but his eyes sparkled with satisfaction because the fire was burning so well.

"Say, Mitsuko," the cameraman said to J's wife, "let's build up the fire and use it to shoot the cut for the introduction to hell."

J

"Fine, if we can put it together making a negative with only the fire in natural colors," Mitsuko enthused. "Like in the Roger Vadim vampire movie, although of course that was blood." She handed each of them a glass and asked if they wanted gin or whisky.

"I'll think about the system; gin for me, please," the cameraman said to J's wife in a lowered voice. It was a voice that could have been meant for a lover.

The subject of their movie was *The Inferno*. When the young poet heard from J and Mitsuko that they were thinking of making a short film about hell, he'd had a sense of dislocation. The impression he'd received at Mitsuko's wedding reception was anything but hellish. Mitsuko had seemed happy after the wedding. She'd garnered the flowers of this earthly paradise, the Jaguar and the Arriflex. The husband also seemed happy to have won such a happy wife. So he couldn't understand why J and his wife would insist on hell. And they were all past the age for girlish tastes. The poet couldn't help suspecting that, even when he'd finished writing the commentary to this film, he still wouldn't understand why hell was necessary. Still, for an instant, when the cameraman turned off the light in the room to measure the effect the fire would have on his film, the poet was seized by the feeling that, in the small fire in the fireplace, he could hear the echoes of his own private hell.

J's sister, the twenty-seven-year-old sculptor, crouched behind the circle of chairs where the others were sitting and started an old-fashioned phonograph. With the room illuminated only by the light from the fireplace, the spot where she was kneeling was like a dark valley. At last, Bach's Partita in B-flat major began to sound through the room—tense, uncertain, but for all that, sweet. The sound was very low and delicate. The record was one of a set from Dinu Lipatti's final concert. They would probably use it as the music for their *Inferno* film. At the recital where this recording was made, Lipatti's health had been almost as bad as it could possibly be; it was his last performance. He had died two months later, while listening to Beethoven's Concerto No. 4 in F-minor.

"The picture over the fireplace is a lot like the one Mitsuko showed to Keiko and me," the young poet said. None of the other six was exactly concentrating on Lipatti, but of the entire group, the poet was the least sensitive to the music.

"It's by the same painter. A Belgian."

"So, I come walking in naked like this, with only my breasts hidden by something that looks like ribbons?" Keiko asked.

"That's right. We have two Roman-style nude statues in the garden, and I want you to come walking in between them. Boy will be standing in the foreground, nude and facing the other way. We're shooting in pan focus, so of course Boy has to do it right too."

"My hair's not that nice," the eighteen-year-old jazz singer said frankly.

The painting was a reproduction of a work by the sur-

J

realist Delvaux, in which several elegant women with lovely pubic hair and an air of abstraction are walking through an eternally quiet landscape in the style of de Chirico. The other six could also plainly feel why the naked bodies of the women in the painting embarrassed Keiko. Their pubic hair was an incomparably beautiful chestnut brown, like a shade of bronze.

The seven, this time including J's sister, had rediscovered the drunkenness they'd felt in the Jaguar. They could still feel the dusk-till-midnight car trip in their legs, from the hips on down, and the tiredness accelerated their intoxication. For the jazz singer, the warmth of the fireplace was an immediate excuse for getting undressed. The dark wine-colored satin dress was like a chicken that had died at her feet. Eventually she would strip off her underwear as well. If this eighteen-year-old had a single quality that made her human, it was her exhibitionism. Nobody took Keiko Sawa for a narcissist. To be perfectly truthful, her body was meager and immature. The young poet thought that she had probably become an exhibitionist because J once told her she looked better naked than with her clothes on. J had the power to influence her. It irritated her that everybody was silently staring at the picture above the fireplace. "If I have to, I'll get a wig that looks like a mouse and tie it to my belly," she said. But then she felt that the other six were paying even less attention to her than before, and she started drinking down the strong gin like water.

"Whereabouts does the sun come up this season, J?" the cameraman asked.

"That's a good question." J had no idea.

"It must come up over the ocean. So Keiko should come walking out between the statues and catch the sunlight from the front, on the left side of her body. She'll throw a long shadow out behind her to the right. The sun will hit Boy's head, shoulders, and side, so his profile will be terribly blackish. We'll set up the camera one meter behind him."

"That's it," the cameraman said to Mitsuko. "I'd like to do the shooting in the morning while the sun still feels like it's lower than we are, so I want to be finished by six."

"Keiko, don't start laughing or anything. This is the crucial scene, so you have to keep a straight face, even if it feels itchy out there in your bare feet."

The jazz singer didn't try to answer. She bent down and took off her underwear. Then she grasped her glass of gin, lemon, and sugar with both hands, like a squirrel holding a walnut, and adjusted herself in the chair with her knees pulled up in front of her. Everybody was resigned to the fact that any attempt at serious conversation with her would now be a waste of time. Her seat was next to J's, which was at the far right of the row of chairs. She and J, who were both too drunk and sleepy to give anything but vague answers, became isolated from the rest. While the other five went on talking about the film, with Mitsuko at the center of the group, Keiko Sawa's naked body gradually wriggled itself to the right, toward J. Putting her thin, bare back and buttocks up as a barricade, she cut herself and J off from the circle of friends. Someone had probably arranged these two chairs to be a little separate from the other five. Everybody knew that J and the jazz singer would sit there.

"The scene where the naked girl comes out between the statues, is that supposed to be a landscape in hell?" the young poet asked Mitsuko. He had to prepare to write his commentary. "Or is it before the fall into hell?"

"It's one of the shots in hell. Isn't that obvious? There aren't any other locations! Haven't I already explained that again and again?"

"A naked girl strolling past a couple of statues with her beautiful pubic hair exposed to the sun—doesn't feel very much like something out of hell to me."

"You're just frustrated."

The young poet let out a sigh of reproach. It's not going to help anything, he thought, consoling himself, no matter what I think about the mental hell of this rich couple or anything else.

The supply of wood in the fireplace had shrunk to almost nothing. The cameraman bent over, with his liquor glass still in his hand, and raked the fire with a poker, trying to get it burning again, but without much effect. The air in the room was warm enough, but they all had what might be called an atmospherical need for a fiercely blazing fire in the fireplace.

"Mitsuko, dear, isn't there any more firewood?" the cameraman asked, turning up his big, round face. In the glow of the fireplace, it was an ugly color like red copper and engorged with blood from his awkward position.

"Of course there is. It should be stacked just outside the kitchen. Assuming it wasn't stolen by those people from the village."

"'Stolen' sounds like your paranoia talking again, Mitsuko," the young actor said. "When that art book of yours disappeared not so long ago you were absolutely convinced that I'd stolen it. It was your paranoia that made you say that, Mitsuko."

"It is no such thing. Boy, even J knows that you've stolen things from our house and sold them. If we take you into our home it's because we don't care if you're a kleptomaniac. If you didn't steal from us what would you do for pocket money?"

The young actor was furious; his entire face turned purple, his eyes filled with tears, his lips quivered. But that was his best acting trick. It wasn't enough to move the others this time.

"What! That's really too much. Do you think you can say anything you want and it's all right, Mitsuko?" the actor said in a tearful voice. Suddenly he stood up and went to the phonograph.

They had all noticed a long time ago that the Lipatti record was over, but they'd ignored it. They'd been listening to the meaningless, fidgety noise of the needle as if it were the wind. The actor put on another record without bothering to look at the jacket. It turned out to be Dixieland jazz.

"Come on and let's dance, Mitsuko," the young actor

said miserably. That was the sort of young man he was—irresolute, with no grip on his emotions.

"No thanks, Boy," Mitsuko said. She was in a bad mood. J's sister, the sculptor, had had enough and stood up.

The young actor and the sculptor started dancing a Charleston. Almost instantly the actor's face, which was too young for his twenty years, beamed with happiness. While they danced, the twenty-seven-year-old woman wiped the remaining traces of tears from his cheeks with her palm. The actor caught her arm, wrapped it around his neck, and pressed himself against her. Now they were dancing in a different style.

"Why don't you stop dancing and bring in some firewood?" Mitsuko said.

"No thanks, Mitsuko darling," the actor said spitefully, making the woman in his arms laugh.

"I'll go and get it," the young poet said. "Do I need a key to get out of the kitchen?"

"The key is in the lock, I think."

Staggering drunkenly, the young poet passed J and the jazz singer, who were sitting shoulder to shoulder in deep silence, and circled around the dancing actor and woman. The fire in the fireplace cast unsteady shadows, upsetting his balance even more. He stumbled when he stepped on his own trembling shadow. When he reached the sofa that they'd turned toward the wall, he thought that somebody was sure to be having sex there, since that's what always happened when he came to one of J's parties. He pushed

open the door in the seaward corner of the wall where
they'd put the sofa and went out. Now he was in the
entrance hall where they'd climbed up the ladder. The stair-
case to the second floor, the bathroom with toilet, and the
door to the kitchen were all there. He pushed the switch
beside the kitchen door and opened it.

The midnight summer air wrapped itself around him,
its touch cold, rough, and yet somehow sweet. The door
from the kitchen into the garden was open and swayed
slightly in the breeze, but nothing about it made him suspicious. He drank some water that was dripping from the tap
and, still barefoot, stepped out onto the lawn. The grass had
grown, and it was hard to estimate the actual ground level.
The young poet gave a cry of profound fear. Then he fell flat
on his face. Possibly he had screamed at the memory of the
steep slope that rose straight up from the sea. But he buried
his face in the thick growth of the lawn, soaking himself
from cheek to throat as though he were swimming in the
dew-drenched grass. He laughed and thought, I'm really
drunk, and just lay there for a few moments without moving. Then he slowly got to his knees, urinated, and went
back to the main hall with an armload of firewood.

The young actor and the woman were embracing and
kissing as they danced. Again the needle was stuck at the end
of the record, but they didn't seem to care. J and the naked
girl were still in the same position, as far as the poet could
see from behind. The cameraman and Mitsuko were sitting
on their knees facing each other in front of the fire and

J

studying the script. The young poet put the firewood down beside them. While the cameraman was building a new fire, he took a fresh glass of liquor from Mitsuko and settled himself in a chair.

"Haven't you got a cut on your cheek? It's stained with blood," Mitsuko said when she came back to the chair beside him.

"I fell down. But I wonder how I got cut."

"You poor thing! You don't even remember?"

"The kitchen door was open to the outside."

"That's not possible," Mitsuko said. She stretched out her neck, which seemed terribly long, and licked the blood from his cheek with her warm tongue. He smelled alcohol and felt disgust, as well as a sudden desire. It was this desire that made him look in J's direction. He felt confused.

The jazz singer's naked back was turned to the young poet. Her head and shoulders rested on J. Her right hand was under J's buttocks and her left hand on his groin. The fingertips of her left hand were extended across J's stiff penis, which made the front of his trousers bulge. J was half sleeping and half smiling. They were undoubtedly locked in the private chamber of a relationship only big enough for two. Suddenly the smell of the naked girl's sex was obvious, even with the odor of the fresh firewood smoldering in the fireplace. Terribly upset, as though caught in a panic, the young poet prayed that J's wife wouldn't notice. He was angered by the obtuseness of the jazz singer. Naturally, he also detested J.

"Let's spread out this wet wood around the fire so it

can dry. Come on, give me a hand," the cameraman said.
Mitsuko and the young poet got down on their knees like
cats and started to help.

At that moment, the naked girl and J stood up behind
them with their arms still entwined and, without releasing
each other, slowly crossed the room and went upstairs. The
young poet was beginning to dread seeing the face of J's
wife. It wasn't the first time something like this had happened. It was just that the young poet was the only one who
couldn't get used to it. But then, the cameraman hadn't gotten completely used to it either. He suggested a new game.

"Mitsuko darling, shall we listen to that tape? If Keiko
were here she'd get mad. Now's the time, don't you think?"

"Fine by me. But Keiko doesn't mind if we use it for
sound effects in the movie, you know," Mitsuko answered
with exaggerated composure. Drunkenness had made her
eyes bloodshot and her cheeks puffy.

The cameraman handled the portable recorder and the
tapes they'd brought in from the Jaguar. No matter where he
was, his actions were always meant to show off his skills as
an engineer. It was his way of confirming to himself that he
actually was the desirable being he should have become. The
caramel-colored tape turned quietly in the glow of the new
fire. At first it didn't produce any sound. The young actor
and the woman were still in each other's arms with their bellies pressed together, but they'd left off kissing and had cast
down their eyes. Each of them was staring intently at the
tape. As long as the tape was silent, the rough breathing of

the sculptor was the only sound in the room. Her breath continued to boil up like foam. From the second floor they could hear the sound of something soft and heavy moving ever so slightly. Then the sound became vague.

Suddenly, a young girl was heard reading a translation of a poem by Baudelaire, "Invitation to a Journey." The quality of the voice was somehow different, but they knew instantly that it was Keiko Sawa. It was closer to her speaking voice than her singing voice, but it was closer still to the voice of an eighteen-year-old girl babbling in excitement. It was a monotonous recitation, a meandering reading of the same one poem repeated as if it were a pronunciation exercise. The tape continued like that for ten minutes. On and on—the recitation was the same translation of the same poem. But then something hidden in the depths of the girl's voice began to change. Was she drunk? The young poet was frankly suspicious, because the jazz singer was almost always drunk. Suddenly he realized that the woman reciting the poem was sexually aroused. There was something feverish in her voice, a dry, infantile quaver, something shrill and thin as it slowly, precariously gathered speed. Occasionally there were ill-timed, unbalanced interruptions. The girl did her best to hold out and continue her performance. She was fighting with an inner resistance, trying to maintain the equilibrium in her voice. She also seemed angry and defiant. For a moment, it was touching. Then the meaningless voice began to get lost in the recitation of the poem. It was the voice of a long-distance runner, singing as she ran. The singer began to gasp, and then she tried to hold out till the end. Ah, ah, the voice flowed out of the caramel-colored tape. Ah, ah. There, there is only order and beauty and luxury, peace and pleasure, and nothing else. Ah, ah, order and beauty and, luxury, peace and, ah, ah! Pleasure and nothing else, ah, ah! Nothing else, ah!

The sensation was like that of a weak tree standing against a flood, trembling, forced to bend as it sinks beneath the water. The voice was resisting in utter despair. Then, unexpectedly, the tree was swallowed up by the flow and was itself transformed into the moment of force of the floodwaters. Ah, ah!

The girl was broken; she cried out and suddenly began to sob. Ah, order and beauty and, ah! That was clearly her final, desperate struggle. The young poet's eyes filled with tears. Then the voice rose explosively, with crude violence. Ah, ah, oh! J! Ah, J, J!

The young poet was stunned. He looked hard at Mitsuko. The tape made a rustling noise as it began to run loose around the reel. Mitsuko bent down and pressed the stop button. All sound was lost in a vague silence. The second floor was quiet too now. The twenty-year-old actor began to snicker.

"The supporting actor on that tape wasn't J, it was me!" he said, his voice breaking with laughter.

"Yes, of course," Mitsuko said, raising her head, as though to answer her old classmate, who was staring at her.

"It wasn't J, it was me!" the actor repeated in triumph

to the sculptor, who was still in his arms. "All the way I didn't make a sound, and I got her that excited!"

"You are a bastard, a real scoundrel!" the sculptor said, the blood rising to her face. Her wide-mouthed laughter showed the red tunnel of her throat.

"I want to use the last three minutes for the title soundtrack," Mitsuko said.

"Ah," the young poet said, feeling strangely as though he'd lost his strength completely. He pushed himself against the straight back of the chair and closed his eyes.

"You know that long slope that goes down to the bay," Mitsuko said, starting to talk with the cameraman. To her and the cameraman, the tape was probably no longer particularly exciting. Possibly the two of them had even been present to witness the recording.

"On the other side or this side?"

"On this side. When J was a child, he saw a truck hit an old man on that hill. The wheels ran over the man's stomach and killed him, and the dog that was with the man lapped up the blood from his master's belly. It acted like it was crazy with joy."

"Crazy with sorrow?" the cameraman asked, with a discrimination that would be expected of a middle-aged man.

"No, crazy with joy."

"What kind of dog was it?"

"A Doberman pup."

"I see!"

"That story may only be one of J's childhood fantasies,

since after all there's a Czech children's story about a dog drinking blood, and I think J might have read it."

"How does it go?"

"When Christ died, a dog lapped up his blood, so the dog was also able to go to heaven."

"The dog could no longer go to heaven?" the cameraman asked.

"The dog could also go to heaven."

"Then we can't use it for this movie."

"That's true," Mitsuko said.

"Aren't you hungry? Let's have the chicken we brought. Then I'm going to get a little sleep."

J's wife brought the oil-paper package of baked chicken and a bottle of sauce from the baggage that also had the 16-millimeter camera packed in it. J's sister had made the sauce that afternoon using plenty of lemon and garlic.

"You boys having some chicken too?"

"I'll have some," the young actor's voice said from the sofa beside the far wall.

"Me too," J's sister announced with a shout, and then suddenly gave a shriek of laughter.

"I'm eating too," the young poet said. He opened his eyes and was dazzled by the faint light of the fire. Everybody downstairs felt hungry.

When the five had gathered in front of the fireplace and started to eat the baked chicken, Boy turned to the others, including J's sister, and raised his voice as though it should be heard, continuing the conversation he'd been having on the sofa. In dead earnest he expressed his disbelief: "Nineteen and impotent! It's impossible."

"It is possible. In fact, I've seen it. My English friend was like that," J's sister laughed, once again letting them look right down her throat. It was a red frightening dark hole.

"Was he a pervert?"

"No."

"Well, it must have been terrible for the woman. I feel sorry for her."

"The woman you're talking about was me," the sculptor said merrily. "Boy, are you still hard? You can give that woman some company!"

Everybody laughed at the young actor. He was constantly the object of this kind of sadistic coddling. And he let himself in for it.

"A French girlfriend of mine gave me some advice. The three of us discussed it. She even checked my boyfriend's parts for me, to make sure he wasn't like young Louis XVI."

"Shit! I'm no good in history, so let's not talk about Louis XVI."

"Anyway, there was nothing wrong with him. My girlfriend explained it this way: if my lover was impotent, it wasn't the responsibility of the young Englishman alone. She related it to the mathematical fact that, in sex between two people, the range of mutual stimulation is limited. So shouldn't sex with three or more people be much more exciting? That's what she said."

They all laughed. J's sister stopped laughing first and said, "So my French girlfriend got into bed and the three of us slept together. In the end our nineteen-year-old performed like a champion. And we all lived happily ever after!"

"But you didn't really enjoy it, did you?"

"Why not?" the twenty-seven-year old sculptor said. Her freezing contempt silenced the young actor.

At that moment, the jazz singer returned to the room. Keiko Sawa was wrapped in a summer blanket from her breasts to her underbelly. Now that she was covered by a blanket, the others turned their eyes away from her more than when she'd been completely naked. The blanket didn't leave the slightest room for doubt about what she and J had just been doing. But she herself was indifferent to such psychological processes.

"How nasty," she said. "Eating without us." She sounded dissatisfied.

"There's plenty left," Mitsuko said.

"J wants you to come upstairs."

"Why?" Mitsuko said coolly.

"We think somebody's watching us, on the second floor! We both felt it. Especially me. I saw a pair of little eyes at the door. So J wasn't any good. In the end, it just didn't happen."

"Me too!" the young actor shouted. "I saw two little eyes looking at us from the shadow of the door to the kitchen. Didn't I just tell you so?"

"You liar. I didn't see anything," J's sister said, laughing and showing her red throat once more.

J

"I also had the feeling somebody was watching us," the cameraman said seriously. "Just a little while ago, when we were listening to Keiko's tape."

The young poet began to feel as though he too had been conscious all along of eyes behind his back. Then he recalled that the kitchen door had been open to the outside when he went to get the firewood. But then he hadn't been particularly suspicious about it. In his mind it was J, waiting upstairs for his wife, who had begun to grow into an overwhelming menace.

"But after all, isn't it true that when a person feels that somebody is watching him, you can always discover a ghost looking at that person? Isn't human consciousness made that way? That's what they call 'the eyes of God' or 'the eyes of the Devil.' When I'm hysterical, I can see eyes like that even in pitch darkness," the sculptor said.

"So even I am hysterical?" the middle-aged cameraman said.

"When I studied philosophy at the Sorbonne . . . "

"That's enough now, talking about philosophy! Just stop it," the young actor said. The sculptor didn't react to his sudden rough language, which gave the others a general understanding of the kind of caresses J's sister and the actor had been exchanging on the sofa a moment before.

"Well, I'm going to have some chicken, so forget about hysterical eyes for a little while," the jazz singer said. She picked up a big chicken wing and started to eat. Her naked breasts were smeared with garlic sauce.

"Go up to J," the jazz singer urged. "Nothing is working with me, and I'm tired." She bit into the chicken with her big white teeth.

Mitsuko shook her head vaguely, and then, with the sad, incoherent eyes of a drowning cat, looked at the young poet. The young poet returned her look. Drink had made him hot, dull, and sluggish, but a single core had formed within him, a core of passion that sparkled clear and distinct. If Mitsuko doesn't go to J, I'm going to lure her away and hide her somewhere, he thought. Don't let her go to him, he prayed. But where can we go? If only these four drunks would all just drop off to sleep . . .

Just then they heard J cry out upstairs. His irritating, urgent-sounding voice called for Mitsuko again and again. The poet burst out in a fit of laughter. Mitsuko slowly stood up. She kept her eyes on the young poet. He stood up too, and they crossed the hall together, walking shoulder to shoulder. They closed the door behind them, and for an instant the two old classmates held each other in the narrow space between the bathroom, kitchen, and stairs. He pressed his hand between the small, naked buttocks under J's wife's skirt. His finger reached her hot, wet eye. Through the poet's trousers, J's wife clutched his madly erect cock.

Seized by desire, the young poet whispered, "Let's hide somewhere, let's go away."

"But where?" a hoarse voice answered, as caught up by desire as him. "Where can we go?"

Feeling cornered, the poet tried to think. Where could

J

they go indeed? Upstairs J was waiting, already out of patience; thirsty people would be coming into the kitchen to drink, one after the other; and every ten minutes there'd be somebody in the bathroom to relieve himself . . .

"The Jaguar?" the young poet said. As the idea came to him, he was seized by a feeling of hope. "Let's hide in the Jaguar."

"J's sister has the key," Mitsuko said, nipping his hope in the bud.

"Let's run away from this house. I'll save you from J. Let's just go!"

"We're just drunk," Mitsuko said. "This isn't love. It's only desire that makes you want to go somewhere." Mitsuko's hand, which had been clutching his sex, now dangled limply between his pants legs.

J called again from the second floor. Mitsuko twisted herself free of the young poet's arms, brushed past him, and went galloping up the stairs. Looking after her, he saw her pale, ugly profile and realized that his words had frightened her off. He was frightened too, frightened by the image of a bitter future with Mitsuko, after she'd lost the ambition to make movies. She's right, he thought. We are just drunk. It isn't love, it's only desire that makes me want to run away with her. He opened the bathroom door and stumbled in. As he was spreading his legs and urinating, he looked down, and the tears that had remained pent up in his eyes until now dripped down, wetting his heavy penis. He thought that was funny and smiled. Then he was captured by a solitary desire that had no connection whatsoever with Mitsuko. As he persistently masturbated, he groped after the slightest clue to an orgasm in the lower depths of the extreme insensibility brought on by drunkenness. When he finally came, the semen dripped like blood, only to fall like thick snow into the beerish froth of tears and piss. He groaned without pleasure. Already he was thinking more about J than Mitsuko. He felt friendship for J. J would probably reduce the desire that he'd aroused in Mitsuko to a bitter ashen broth. He vaguely connected J, Mitsuko, and then himself with the image of the threesome in J's sister's recollection. He felt that fantasy to be altogether harmonious and satisfying. For the first time he felt comfortably at home in J's world. He felt that he, like the jazz singer and the young actor, had surrendered to the mighty J, but he didn't experience any feeling of humiliation. He tucked his rapidly wilting penis into his trousers and pulled the chain to flush the toilet. He sat down on the bathtub beside him, motionless. It was getting harder and harder not to fall asleep. He lay down in the empty tub. He started to sleep, but in the instant before the young poet drifted off, he felt that he was a happy dead man in his coffin. He should write about it in a poem, he thought. He also thought he'd write about the pair of limpid eyes that he could see now, seeming to watch him from the far side of the open door as he lay in the bathtub . . .

J

~

In the darkness, Mitsuko felt that J was finally beginning to climb the slope toward ejaculation. She caressed his anus and raised her voice in boyish powerful groans to encourage him. The crystal clear, perfectly composed feeling she had now reminded her of times when, as a child, she would swim in the river and slip to the bottom, lying on her back and looking up at the surface of the water as it glittered in the sunlight. She didn't feel the slightest pleasure. J's spasms were accompanied by a slightly embarrassed cry. With the composure of a nurse, Mitsuko patiently accepted J's sweaty body and the weight he now rested on her. From the length of his ejaculation, it was clear that Keiko hadn't been lying. She also knew that J didn't particularly like having intercourse with Keiko. In his sex with her, J only faked enthusiasm. Mitsuko could also guess why that was. It seemed to justify the fact that Mitsuko herself always feigned excitement when she was having intercourse with J. But then why did J so stubbornly insist on sex with her and Keiko? Mitsuko had seldom thought deeply about it, and she certainly had never gotten to the bottom of the problem. A vague presentiment of the frightening answer she would find had made her leave the question alone. She felt that the way J insisted on having a woman was probably, in its essence, a lie.

J had quietly collapsed at Mitsuko's side and, in the darkness, had turned onto his back in the same position as Mitsuko. Their naked bodies lay arranged together in the dark. They listened to the sound of each other's breathing. Both had their eyes wide open. When the sweat began to chill them, their naked legs worked together to pull the blanket over their bodies. All the while they remained silent. Downstairs they could hear the echoing laughter of Keiko, the actor, and J's sister. They could not hear the voices of the cameraman and the young poet . . .

"Instead of a fake orgasm, don't you ever want to try for the real thing?" J said suddenly.

"That's not important to me. My real orgasm is film," Mitsuko said. It felt like they'd had this husband-and-wife conversation a hundred times before.

"But tonight, for the first time, you were headed for the real thing."

"It was no such thing. It can't happen." She was genuinely shocked and practically paralyzed with fear. She believed that frigidity was the most essential element of her free existence.

"But you were excited."

"I wasn't. I tell you it's not possible."

"If that's the way you want it, okay. I'm going to sleep," J said. Then he was silent.

Mitsuko had lost her sense of certainty. That's right—it must be like J said. I was excited, she thought. Mitsuko had had sex with her old classmate before, but when the poet

J

held her outside the door, she'd suddenly discovered a new self that was in an orbit leading toward orgasm. Whenever J held her, no matter what she did to entice him, his fingers were incapable of even imitating the movement of the poet's fingers in that one moment. What Mitsuko had felt dimly, when the poet's fingers went instantly and without hesitation to her sex, was not a lie, but the action of a person who wants a woman. That was the opposite of J. For a moment she had felt that she might abandon filmmaking and run off into the darkness outside the mountain house with her old lover, the poet. Suddenly she had been struck by a deep fear. So she rejected the path of destruction which led to the orgasm inside her, rejected the young poet, and decided to return to film, which was her one and only passion. That was why, pale and trembling, she'd gone up the stairs. When she reached that dark room, which was still redolent of the jazz singer's body and started to have intercourse with her husband, who was waiting in the unpleasantly warm bed, she had felt as though she'd completely conquered her moment of vacillation.

For Mitsuko, J was the ideal husband. He gave her everything she needed to make a film, and he always let her stay inside herself. She was trying to become a truly liberated female artist, and for that, she had to be free of all the constraints that constitute womanhood. She had to reject every temptation that might turn her firm insides into an unstable viscous gruel. Her orgasm as a woman would destroy her fundamental antifeminine rights as a filmmaker. Mitsuko had resolved not to fall into that trap. She thought she had also succeeded in her efforts to establish her freedom from the poison of female jealousy; but if one passing caress from the young poet could stir her as much as that, where was she supposed to go from here? Since her husband was sleeping beside her, Mitsuko stiffened her body so that he wouldn't notice as she cried a few tears. Several times while they were having sex, J had screwed his head around and said that a pair of eyes were watching them from somewhere. She tried to urge him on, saying, "No, J, there's nobody watching us, doesn't this feel good, just relax now, let it happen, there's nobody and nothing watching." But she too felt like someone was watching them. Were those the eyes of the evil spirit who wanted to see the moment of her defeat—when, like a silly woman, she would feel the orgasm even a dog can feel, when she would give up her passion for the great work of creating an avant-garde film just for the dirty instinct of sex? Sobbing, Mitsuko went to sleep . . .

J was liberated. While his wife was sobbing, he lay on his back, naked, breathing only slightly. Like a traveler who encounters a bear, he pretended to be dead, partly out of fear and partly as a strategy. He even wished he had gills he could breathe through. Two years before, the cameraman, who'd been a friend since childhood, had introduced him to a young woman who aspired to be a film director. She was just out of school and had a temporary job in the production studio where the cameraman was making educational films. She was wearing jeans and had her dirty hair pulled back in

J

a knot that she tied with a rubber band. There was something pathetic and young about her; she had a manic look in her eyes. Sexually the young woman was completely free, but because she was frigid, she didn't attach any particular importance to intercourse. All her passion was bent toward her dream of making a film. A year later, J and the girl got married. From that time forward, he had pursued his grand, untiring, insidious project. J had wanted to create a private sexual microcosm, with himself at its center. But J dreaded scandal, a dread of what was virtually the life's blood of the society in which his family moved. Unlike his sister, with her foolhardy courage, J possessed the cowardly heart of a rabbit. After the death of his first wife, he'd become incapable of dealing in any way with the real world. Instead, he became even more firmly attached to his private sexual microcosm, like an oyster clinging to a rock. That, he felt, was the one road to meaning in his life.

Before they'd been married a year, J himself had already intimated to Mitsuko that he was a person who could not find satisfaction in perfectly ordinary sexual intercourse. Mitsuko had realized that there was a connection between his orgasm and his anus, which tapered like the end of a lemon, and had made it a regular habit to caress him there. She had also accepted it when J led the jazz singer into the sexual world of their marriage. She became another one of their habits. Mitsuko had tried to understand that J felt incomplete during intercourse. But the next step would be an extremely difficult one.

"Am I finally to reach the complete fulfillment of my sexual world?" J thought blankly. He was lost in a fog of insecurity and despair. Countless nights he'd passed the last minutes before the darkness of sleep drenched in this suffocating fog, permeated by a sense of exhaustion. Possibly it was a fog that would not completely clear until his difficult sexual world was complete. Bringing the young actor into their sexual world, to take the place of the jazz singer, would be the final step. His wife had shown no particular shock when the eighteen-year-old girl joined them, but was it really possible that she would show no more shock when a twenty-year-old boy slipped into their bed? J had gradually led his wife to the point where she was free of her prejudice against homosexuality. She no longer reacted when he invited homosexuals to their parties. But it would take a leap over a chasm of the greatest width and depth for her to enter a bed where her own husband was already conjoined in sex with another man. There was no question about that. "Will I be able to plant the delusion in my wife's head that I am making her take that great leap for no other reason than to free her from her frigidity?" He would remain hopeful if, until the faraway day when that could be accomplished, she would do him the favor of devoting herself solely to film, with no interest in an easy orgasm.

His wife breathed with difficulty as she slept. J recalled the winter night, just before dawn, when his first wife had killed herself. She and J were sleeping in the same bed when suddenly he noticed that there was something wrong with

J

her breathing. His wife had discovered that he was having a homosexual affair with his sister's foreign teacher. J was living for the day when he could recover completely from the deep fear that he had felt in bed on that predawn winter night. He thought that he would for the first time be able to liberate himself from his dead first wife when his second wife accepted his sexual microcosm. Why? Now that he could no longer make amends to his dead wife, he would by an inverse process convert his feeling of sin into legimate self-defense. That would mean nothing more or less than the restoration of peace in his heart.

J was sleeping like a ghost in the heart of a pure blackness, a tar-like sleep. He knew, of course, that he was no different from a cornered criminal ready to fight. That was why, in the dark abyss of sleep, he couldn't help but notice the glitter of the accusing pair of eyes that he had felt watching him earlier. He slept an anxious sleep, threatened from the bottom of his heart . . .

In the main room the cameraman was sleeping in front of the fireplace. He was curled up like a fetus, his body drawn in to the very limit. He gave a much older, sullenly friendless impression than when he was awake and mingling with the others. His sleep was a total rejection of the others. It wasn't only in his company that he was an isolated being out of harmony with the world. As long as he lived in this world, there would probably never be an instant when he lived in harmony with it. Anyone who saw the forty-year-old man sleeping that night, like an animal, locked up inside his ego, would have wondered about the purpose of his being there, surrounded by these young men and women.

The jazz singer was still sitting on the floor beside the cameraman with her arms around her naked knees, about to gulp down the last of the gin-and-tonic. Unsatisfying sex with J had created a hard body of resistance inside her that was unpleasant. She was drinking strong liquor because she wanted to dissolve it and excrete it. She had already drunk too much. Drunkenness and drowsiness made a comical red nebula wheel around inside her small eighteen-year-old head. The glass slipped from her hands like sand. She gave a forced yawn and tried to stand, but there was no way that she was going to get up. She growled angrily at her legs and staggered as she made another unavailing effort to rise.

"Who was better, me or the foreigner?" the boy's coquettish voice repeated, low and insistent, from the sofa by the wall. "Well, who was better, me or the foreigner?"

"When I was overseas, I didn't know what to do if I got pregnant. I was scared to death at the thought of it. I was still a child then," the sculptor finally answered, sounding sleepy.

"But who was better, me or the foreigner?" the twenty-year-old actor went on saying in a sing-song voice.

The jazz singer slowly started to walk to the door. By the time she had passed the sofa, the sculptor and the young actor had already gone to sleep. The jazz singer opened the door and closed it again. Then, after having trouble telling which was the bathroom door and which was the kitchen's, she went into the bathroom. She was singing a Negro song

J

in a low voice, but it came back to her more like the buzzing of a bee's wings. Half sleeping, she sat down on the toilet and took a languid piss. The smell of urine and alcohol rose up around her like the steam of a hot shower.

A smallish moving body darkened the jazz singer's closed eyelids for an instant, like the shadow of a bird flickering past. Still in the act of urinating, the eighteen-year-old girl opened her enraptured eyes. The small presence stopped right in front of her, as though suspended, and looked at her with glittering eyes. Oh, it's you! Those eyes! Without raising her voice, she screamed in the back of her throat. In an instant the eyes jumped nimbly behind her back. Because she was too drunk, and too sleepy, her gaze couldn't follow them. The creature had seemed like a baby monkey, and it had seemed like a small god, like a traveler's guardian. By the time she finished urinating and slowly got up from the toilet, she'd already forgotten about the intruder. She walked back to the main room like a somnambulist and gradually fell into a deep sleep. A milky light was already beginning to show through the glass door that opened onto the garden. The fire was completely dead. Nobody was awake. The ocean breeze carried the crowings of several cocks up from the bayside village. Without waking up, the sleepers shivered in the early-morning cold . . .

At 4 A.M. the cameraman discovered the tiny ten-year-old intruder sleeping like a bat as he stood against the wall in the dark shadow of the stairs. He tiptoed into the bathroom, squatted like a woman to pee so he wouldn't make any noise, came back the way he'd come, and grabbed the child. It began to struggle frantically as soon as it opened its eyes. The cameraman was stunned and called out to rouse his friends. Grumbling but nonetheless curious, the others woke up—first the young poet, who was asleep in the bath-tub; then the twenty-seven-year-old sculptor and the young actor, who were on top of each other on the sofa; and the jazz singer. Finally J and his wife came downstairs to join them in surrounding the captured child. The cameraman held the child's arms, while the young actor kept it from bit-ing the cameraman. Though the child kicked them both without mercy, they finally managed to carry it into the main room. The other five moved excitedly with them, not breaking the circle. The child was like a little devil. The young poet bent over to hold down its legs but straightaway was kneed in the face. His nose started to bleed. Even though the child was being held by three strong men, it writhed like an eel in stubborn silence. The actor screamed in anger and pain when the child bit his finger. Blood trick-led down the cameraman's cheek. The child seemed mad with anger and frozen with fear. It was like the capture of a small wild animal they'd seen in an animal film from Kenya. The fear that this small animal might drop dead of a heart attack if it continued to rage like this flitted around the heads of its seven captors. An irresistible irritation was gradually rising in the three who were actually holding the child. What should they do now that they had the child? Suddenly, as unnaturally as if a steel spring had snapped in its tiny body, the child stopped all resistance. Then it screamed in a strange tinkling voice stained with the poison of hatred, "But I saw it!" It drenched its upturned little black face with tears, clucked its tongue—hard and sharp as a snake's—against the roof of its mouth, and cried . . .

The seven captors were dumbfounded. In the next instant the child recaptured the appearance of the agile moving body which the jazz singer had seen the night before, not knowing if it was a monkey or a small god. He broke free of the three men's arms, knocked the women down, and dashed toward the wide, still-closed glass door. A sound like the coming of the end of the world filled the room. The seven all closed their eyes. When they opened them again, they saw the boy's small back run into the swirling fog in the still-dark garden beyond the shattered glass door. He was screaming and in tears and probably staining the dew-drenched lawn with blood, since his bare feet were full of glass shards. The night was nearly over, and it seemed that in a short while the fog would continue its retreat as well . . .

Excited and reproachful, the seven stared in silence at the garden where the fog swirled, as though they were looking hard at the surface of a sea where the ripples are subsiding after the fish have been hauled in. Pregnant with dew drops, the early-morning air came blowing in like a wave through the big hole in the shattered door, causing a powerful convection in the room. Their heads were too warm and their lower bodies too cold. The smell of the tide gradually permeated the room. All seven stood as they'd been when the boy escaped, with only their heads turned to the garden where day was breaking, following the after-image of the thing that had disappeared silently into the sea of fog. The film that was recording their movements had stopped there, and the mercury lamp was uselessly flashing a single still image. Only one of them, the jazz singer, broke from the still image and hurried to the back of the room. She'd gone to turn off the light. The room sank back into the depths of night, and they only saw each other's faces, like the black faces of mummies. The glass door, both the broken part and the part still intact, immediately turned a brighter white, as if the door were a wall separating the night in the room from the foggy garden. The others thought the jazz singer would turn the light on again. She must have been too sure that day had broken. But she stood where she was, without moving, her head pressing the wall above the switch.

"Put on the lights. What's the matter with you?" J shouted in a rancorous, frightened voice that was so loud the others all thought they were hearing him speak that way for the first time.

"No, I don't want to. We have to keep it dark!" the eighteen-year-old said vehemently, still facing the other way. Her shoulders began to shake and she started to sob, tumbling down the incline toward hysteria. She was gasping uncontrollably, and her body was writhing. "Ah, ah!" she cried. "We're going to be killed. Those people from the bay will kill us. As soon as they hear what that boy has to say, they'll come to get us! Look what they did to that woman for nothing but adultery . . . "

J

The other six kept their distance from the hysteria, but none was now free from the ominous image of those fishing people who'd spilled onto the flagstone road at midnight to carry out a silent threat . . .

"Let's get away in the Jaguar. Come on, let's get in the Jaguar and get out of here before they come!" The jazz singer was still crying.

"That's no good," J said. "If, as you say, they are mad and want to do something to us, they'll get together right away to block the road by the bay. We won't have a way out."

"Then what do we do?" the hysterical girl sobbed.

"First turn on the light, and we'll worry about it over a leisurely breakfast," J said. He walked over to where the jazz singer was standing. As he pressed the light switch with his left hand, he touched the girl's neck with his right. She let out a short scream, as though she couldn't conceal her revulsion. She brushed his hand away and fell into a crouch. Her forehead was pressed so hard against the wall that it seemed the skin might burst . . .

The six who were watching the singer by the light of the lamp felt uncomfortable and embarrassed. Not looking at one another, they searched for chairs where they could sit or walls to lean against. From his lips to his chin the young poet was covered with blood from his nose. The actor had put his bloody finger into his mouth. The cameraman groaned as he wiped the blood from his cheek. The women weren't hurt as badly as the three bleeding men, but without their makeup, it was impossible to look at their faces in the bright light without a feeling of disgust. They all had slept badly, had hangovers, and were overcome by a feeling of self-abandonment. At the same time they all felt an accelerating mood of meanness and insecurity.

"Why did you have to treat him like that?" J said, blaming the cameraman. "He would've gone back happy if you'd just given him a fountain pen or something."

"He went crazy in my arms before I realized it," the cameraman said, defending himself. Hesitating, he added, "Anyway, it was bound to turn out the way it did. Didn't he say he'd seen us?"

Once again an evil silence, filled with traps even more uncomfortable than before, hung over their heads like the shadow of a plane. That's right, they all thought, he had seen absolutely everything. Then they realized that, until then, nobody in the group of seven had seen or been seen by another person; none of them had even seen themselves.

Standing by the shattered door, J's sister noticed the blood that had been spilled there. The little boy had plunged through the glass like a diver into water. The trail continued to where the balcony met the lawn. Quite a lot of blood had been uselessly spent staining the overgrown summer grass. She wondered how much blood such a small child's body could afford to waste.

She turned and looked hard at J. Then, as if passing judgment on him for raising his head in that embarrassed smile, she said, "He was just an innocent kid, J. He hadn't done anything wrong. If it turns out that he threw himself over the cliff and died, you'll have your second victim."

"Why do you say that?" Mitsuko said in a plaintive voice. She was so shaken that for an instant she'd forgotten the runaway child.

' "Because J has already made one innocent, unsuspecting person kill herself."

"You mean his first wife?" Mitsuko said. "Wasn't she a neurotic who committed suicide?" She turned to J. "How was that your responsibility, J?"

"It was my fault," J said. They were all silent. Only the jazz singer continued to sob, squatting by herself and turned away from the others. She was like a mentally retarded student who is always by herself in the classroom. Her ugly, pathetic sobbing annoyed and angered the others.

"Why?" Mitsuko asked.

"It's a complicated story."

"But it was because of her?" Mitsuko said, finding some small, twinkling sign of hope.

"No, there's more to it than that."

Mitsuko's feeling of despair returned, becoming even deeper than before. "How did she do it?" she asked her husband again and again.

"Didn't you marry me knowing that my first wife had committed suicide? It doesn't concern you." J scrambled into his shell like an egotistical hermit crab, while at the same time falling deeper into despair.

"It does concern her, because you're about to do the same thing again," J's sister said bluntly. "In fact, you've already done the same thing if, at this very minute, that child has gone over the cliff into the ocean like a cut-up bag."

"So it was just me? What that child saw was only me in an act of dirty sex? Didn't he also see plenty of you? Or isn't your sex as dirty as mine?"

"You shameless pig!" the twenty-seven-year-old sculptor said. Her voice was like the hard, trembling cry of a bird, and altogether dark. A wave of tears welled up in her gummy, bloodshot eyes, which were beginning to appear ruined. Still glaring at her brother, she began to cry without a sound.

"What did you do? How did you make your first wife kill herself?" Mitsuko demanded, ignoring her sister-in-law, who continued to sob, her shoulders trembling.

"Someday I'll tell you."

"I want to hear it now," Mitsuko said.

"You'll hear it, and then what will you do? After all, what difference does it make to you? Didn't you marry me just because you wanted to make movies? Now that you're making this avant-garde movie with your silly images of hell, what more do you want from me?"

J tried to defend himself, but his voice wasn't very convincing. He himself felt disgusted with his own voice.

"J, it won't do any good to evade the question." J was surprised when the pale middle-aged cameraman suddenly intervened. J and the cameraman had been friends for nearly ten years, but in all that time J had always been the master of the relationship. Not once had the cameraman risen up against him. J felt terribly threatened at this discovery of a new stranger, in the form of the cameraman.

"I just . . . " J's face turned an unsightly red as he groped for some point of compromise. He had to make the cameraman offer fresh acknowledgment of his decade-long subservience. J had already become as incoherent as a fainthearted, egotistical child.

"J's first wife killed herself because, even after he'd married the poor girl, he kept jumping into bed with that filthy foreign faggot, in broad daylight. She was a genuine innocent. He didn't actually confess to her, but on the other hand, he didn't do very much to make sure she wouldn't find out. J, from the day you married her, you were hoping your wife would kill herself. You knew she'd taken something like a hundred sleeping pills, but you lay there pretending to sleep, just waiting for her to die. J, are you going to keep quiet and try to fool us forever?"

J jumped from his chair and went for the cameraman. The cameraman offered no resistance to J's fist as it hit his cheek. He simply endured, as he became more and more pale and the blood trickled from his lips. Now he was a middle-aged man, totally exhausted. He didn't even raise his voice in pain. In the end, J kept beating him only out of some sense of duty.

"Stop him. Somebody stop him before he beats him to death," Mitsuko screamed in a voice that was sharp as a shriek. Overwhelmed by pain and anger, she sounded like she was being beaten herself.

The young poet got up and seized J from behind. When his hands touched J's right arm, with its clenched fist, and his left shoulder, all the strength went out of J instantly and he became soft as a baby. For a moment, the young poet thought J might collapse. But that didn't happen. He was gasping and his face was crimson, but he remained motionless in the young poet's grasp and offered no resistance. In a cheerless voice, as if he were the one who'd been beaten, he said, "Let me go. Haven't I had enough?"

When the young poet dropped his arms, and stopped holding J, J went back to his chair. He turned his face from the poet, who remained standing by Mitsuko's chair like a guard, glaring at J. J buried his face in his hands and didn't move. It appeared that he too was about to burst into tears, but he didn't accept his defeat so easily. He raised his feverish red monkey's face and glared back at the young poet.

"I know that you've slept with my wife," he said, "and I know that you want her sometimes now. But you come to my place, hiding it all behind that well-mannered silence and smiling face of yours. Now that you're eyeing me like a prosecutor, doesn't that bother you deep down?"

A gloomy silence filled with fierce hostility locked J, Mitsuko, the sculptor, the young poet, and the cameraman each in their private prison cells. They cowered, motionless, inwardly stained with the ink of resentment, distrust, and lost friendship. They grasped in vain for edges of the coil of imaginary friendships which had bound them so intimately the night before, wondering if those edges themselves wouldn't soon melt and vanish like frost. They all felt miserable, alone and forsaken. The jazz singer's sobbing was like a voice that had been wrecked by their combined malice . . .

The twenty-year-old actor, the only one who was free from the hysteria and the chains of malice, still felt he had failed. He was nothing but a dull-witted tough guy, a boy with no imagination and fragile powers of judgment, but nevertheless he still sensed something waiting beneath his physical discomfort and displeasure. And it was something that disturbed him deeply. It got on his nerves, so he wanted somehow to replace the emergence of that strange danger with something completely trivial and conquer that. He looked around restlessly. Then suddenly an idea came to him. He spoke abruptly, breaking the silence.

"I want to take a shower. I want to get in that bath and have a shower. I feel bad. I always have a bath and a shower in the morning after I've been with a woman! My own semen, the leavings from the woman's Bartholin's gland—it all seems like it's plastered to my penis. It's really a nasty feeling."

The young actor knew as well as the others that they'd run out of propane and couldn't use the bathroom. They were all caught by the unpleasant and itching realization that their skin was filthy. The chain of malice was now double-wrapped and colored with physical self-loathing. There was nothing left for the actor but to play the buffoon.

"I feel so nasty, my whole body stinks! It feels like I've got a penis and a vagina both, and both of them smell like shit!"

Of course the other six didn't laugh. The young actor's mood turned even worse, and he felt terribly sad. He felt like a fretful tot. He stood up so violently that he turned over his chair, and walked over to the glass door. He walked like a thief or an adulterer in an extremely stylized classical play, taking care not to cut the soles of his feet on the shards of glass. Suddenly he returned to his everyday voice and called the others over. It was the voice of a crybaby.

"Look! It's them! They're here! Look!"

They all looked round at the garden, where dawn was breaking on the other side of the glass door. The fog had completely cleared, and it was a beautiful summer morning. The slope of overgrown lawn was a single sheet of green outside the door. Sky and sea were invisible, and there were no trees in sight. Here and there in the roughly tended, very thickly-grown lawn, some wild grasses tougher than the lawn made high-backed green humps of a still deeper green. And then there were the two statues. The statue in the foreground was Apollo. His left arm, missing its hand, was extended forward and to the left. The head of the noble youth gazed in the same direction. The relaxed bundle of muscle of his left leg, lifted slightly at the heel, was wet with dew and solemnly cast a faint shadow in the calm light of dawn, before the direct rays of the sun appeared. Only the places where the grape leaf met the insides of his thighs were

J

hidden in thick black shadow. The statue in the background was clearly Zeus. The old man's face was wreathed in a beard and hair in the same style. His eyes opened like two vacant holes that were the only remnants of night left in the green garden, which was now evenly lighted by the faint glow of dawn.

Between the two statues, the fisher folk suddenly appeared to those who were waiting, sitting or standing, in the depths of the main room. They all shivered at the discovery. It was the same group of villagers that had occupied the narrow stone road the night before. Middle-aged women, old people, and children—their faces in the light of dawn seemed plainer, more animal-like, and more shrunken than in the headlights. Had they spent a sleepless night on that road? Had that silent gathering, intended to intimidate and shame the adulterous woman who was stealthily preparing her lonely meal, lasted till daybreak? If, with the exception of those who went out fishing, all the remaining villagers, still indignant, had stayed on the road all night long, did that mean the village of Miminashi Bay was a village of people so nasty that they would disrupt their daily lives for the sake of malice? The seven in the room were again connected in a circle of common fear. Just as the night before a vague affinity had made them take a collective responsibility for the wild party, they were now forced together again in a party of fear and violence that was about to begin. Something like forty fisher folk were silently approaching. They came as close as the front of the balcony.

The seven in the room saw a middle-aged woman with thick hair and dark skin like an Indian and a boy with a bloody cheek emerge from the group as though pushed forward. They all felt like they had entered the final stage. It was already clear that the fisher folk who stood there peeping into the room had the same cruel look in their eyes, the same brutal passion hidden in their souls, as they had shown in front of the house of that miserably oppressed woman. The twenty-year-old actor was overwhelmed and retreated between the chairs of his friends. Would the people outside scream and burst in, crossing the threshold of violence? Would the seven in the room burst into tears and pass out trembling before it came to that? But the seven frightened people in the room didn't do anything. They simply waited while the people from Miminashi Bay, their ankles hidden in the deep grass and their calves wet with dew, positioned themselves to attack . . .

J's sister got up from her chair and stepped forward. The fragments of broken glass crunched under her slippers. She carefully slipped through the dangerous hole in the shattered glass door and went out alone onto the balcony to confront the villagers. The six watching from inside could see that the people of Miminashi Bay were deeply shaken.

"We were worried the boy might have fallen from the cliff and died. He'd been hiding here all night and he crashed through the glass when he ran away. But it looks like he's not hurt too badly," J's sister said. She was haughty to the point of shamelessness as she made this desperate counter-

J

attack. Would her political trap catch these people? Or would the fisher folk of Miminashi Bay sniff out her fragile lie and make of the tiny opening offered by that lie a hand-hold with which to instantly destroy her. The six in the back were seized by anguished doubt.

There was silence and a feeling of urgency in the uncertain outcome of the decision. Wouldn't the boy scream out and crush J's sister's deception? A moment passed. J's sister had won. With her left hand, the Indian-like woman seized the head of the boy, who, with down-turned eyes, was clinging to the left side of her high, fat hip. Then she raised her right hand and hit him above his ear with all her might. It made a sharp sound. A shiver of nausea coursed through the woman on the balcony and the six in the room. The boy fell face down in the grass. The village woman gave him a kick in the buttocks with her sturdy leg. The boy escaped, crawling across the grass like a young animal; then he hurriedly got up and ran away screaming. He cried out his indignation in a teary voice. "I saw! I saw!"

"That little fool, he says he's seen devils, seen killer devils, he says! That little lying fool. What a disgrace!" the woman said. An embarrassed, mean little smile rose to her cheeks. The faces around the woman all relaxed and turned apparently good-natured and impersonal. They'd all become captive to an ambiguous sense of shame and were smiling in confusion . . .

"You don't need to worry about the glass. But could you bring us some fish, as usual? We're here to shoot a movie. There are seven of us, so we'll want a lot, okay?"

"A movie!" There was a commotion of words for a few moments. The people of Miminashi Bay were already completely under the sway of J's sister's trickery.

"That's what we were doing last night, and it's why everybody is up and around so early this morning. We're not here for a holiday!" she said with reproach. She was finishing off her hunted-down enemy, and now seemed full of confidence and even proud of her victory.

The women and old people apologetically defended themselves. The boats that put out fishing from the village on Miminashi Bay were all having a terrible time with bad catches, so those who stayed behind were trying their best to locate and drive out of the bay the evil spirits that must be causing the poor catches. Until the adulteress confessed all her sins and begged for forgiveness in front of them all, they'd keep watching her. When she'd submitted, one evil spirit would be expelled. But there were so many they had to find . . .

The people of Miminashi Bay silently formed a single group again, passed between the statues, and walked down the hill. J's sister came back into the room, slipping as carefully as before through the hole in the broken glass. With the garden behind her, her face was completely black. Only her silhouette, with its downy hair, shone in the green light. She had been majestic and awe-inspiring in front of the fisher folk, but now that she'd come back to the room, she was an unsteady, worn-out, weary, dazed old woman. She turned to the other six and spoke in a thin, hoarse voice.

"I'm going to sleep for a little while. There's nothing you really need me for now, is there?" she said with self-contempt, but also with bad humor that sounded like a challenge. Then she passed between the chairs, crossed the room, opened the door, and disappeared. A few moments later they heard the sound of a door being opened upstairs. It was a different room from the one where J had slept. Nobody spoke or moved, so they could hear J's sister closing the door and then the heavy sound of her falling into bed, probably with her clothes still on. Then the second floor was silent.

"Let's put the camera together," the cameraman said. "If we don't get ready for the shoot, the sun'll be up already." As could be expected, he sounded ill-tempered, but he very clearly wanted to recover what had been destroyed by the talk they'd had earlier. He stood up alone, bent down near the Arriflex case, and started to work. He was silent and rough, as if he were angry, but at the same time there was something sluggish about his manner.

As always, the cameraman's suggestion was a relief to the others. Mitsuko soothed the jazz singer, who was still pale and teary in the aftermath of her attack of hysteria, and tried to convince her that she should get to work. To heighten the photographic effect, the young poet drew a bucket of water and walked across the lawn to wash the skin of the Apollo statue. Usually J was lazy and refused to participate in any job that involved physical labor, but today he washed the statue of Zeus. The young actor cheerfully stripped to

the waist and examined the lawn where the little boy had
fallen after being hit to check whether there was any blood
on the grass. The temperature was already climbing the way
it would on a midsummer's day, and the garden was no
longer cold. After much persuading by Mitsuko, the jazz
singer finally came down to the lawn, completely nude, and
stumbled toward the statues. The eighteen-year-old-girl's
tear-stained childish little face was pale and dark and very
ugly, but her slender naked body was quite erotic and mys-
terious. It would evoke perfectly the surrealist image of a
naked woman in the film. Mitsuko was studying the script
as she stood by the cameraman, who was adjusting the film
equipment. She was pale and ugly. The sea far below was
already giving off the scorching reflection of the sun. The
garden was right at the center of a brilliant summer morning.

"Look, that child lost a tooth here!" the young actor
shouted, sounding concerned. He was holding a small lump in
his right hand. His naked torso turned a rosy color in the light
of the sun, and he was smiling. "He must be hurting pretty
badly! But maybe the pain in his mouth will make him forget
about the pain in his heart!"

J, his wife, the jazz singer, the cameraman, and the
young poet stopped what they were doing. Without moving
or speaking, they all looked at the young actor. Their eyes
were flaming with criticism.

"Well, he'll soon forget about seeing devils while
he's bleeding and trying to cope with the pain, won't
he?" the young actor shouted.

J

They stood there in silence, with no idea what to do. Uncertain and irritated, the young actor went on screaming.

"Well, what's the matter with you all? You look like a bunch of mummies. What is it? Did somebody stop the clock or something?"

Nobody answered. They stood frozen, looking at him. With the child's tooth still clenched in his right hand, the young actor suddenly sank to his knees in the blood-stained grass, bowed his head, chafed his body, and began to cry. "Damn," the twenty-year-old muttered through his tears. "I hate this. Here in this place, naked like this, doing this job— this is no fun at all! Ah, I can't stand this anymore. There must be some fun job for me to do, but, damn, other kids have got them already . . . "

Part Two

IT HAD BEEN ONE MINUTE since the crowded subway train had pulled out of the Diet Station. J and the old man both noticed the young man at the same time. He was about eighteen, well-built, and wore an English trench coat—the kind meant for young people, with clusters of buttons and buckles. Peering out from the collar of his coat, his sweat-drenched face and neck had a white glow. They saw one of the young man's legs as he took a determined step into the densely packed thicket of human bodies. For an instant they saw his bare calf and knee. He was wearing deerskin boots. He seemed thin, but his fleshy neck and head suggested that his weight was well above average. And if he looked thin, it was probably because, apart from the trench coat and boots, he was completely naked.

The subway train was racing along at top speed, shaking like a newspaper boy late for his rounds on a winter morning. The youth took another step forward. Beads of

J

sweat surfaced on his forehead like fish eggs. His body was now fitted snugly against the back and buttocks of a young girl. She had a monstrous growth on her forehead and a smug, upturned nose, but he had approached her from behind. With steely self-control, he sighed quietly, soundlessly, and glanced cautiously around. He had the eyes of a dog too sick even to chase a sewer rat. The fever had erased whatever glimmer of cunning vitality those eyes might still have contained. His small nose, Mongolian in shape, widened heroically as he sniffed for any suspicious scent. About fifteen feet above the passengers' heads lay the bleak evening city in early winter. Ten million people lived there and the young man seemed to know there was not one who would help him in his very personal mission.

He seemed at ease, although dripping with sweat. In his arrogance, he felt completely removed from the world around him. He was deliriously excited, almost fatally aroused, as he let his hard male weapon emerge from a small slit in a hidden pocket of his coat. He began to rub it lovingly, anxiously, determinedly, against the girl's buttocks through her orange coat; and an innocuous, saintly smile began to curl his lips, then spread gradually across his entire face . . .

J and his elderly but well-built friend stood shoulder to shoulder as they watched this scene. The tension was so unbearable that both felt an urge to close their eyes. The old man was afraid he'd have a heart attack. The train pulled into the next station and stopped, disgorged some people, sucked in others, and started again. Hoping the youth had disappeared, J and the old man looked toward the place where he'd been standing. The jungle of passengers was less dense than before, but they discovered the young man still in action. To make matters worse, he was about to have an orgasm, inevitable as death itself. Suddenly, not only J and his friend, but everyone on the train, seemed to open their eyes wide and focus on the young man with a terrible, united force. Under this glare of strangers' eyes, he climaxed. At that moment, a powerfully-built middle-aged man, who'd been standing next to J and the old man, reached out and grabbed the collar of the young man's trench coat as if he were about to rip it off his back. J and the old man swallowed hard and sighed.

"He went too far," J whispered in the old man's bulbous ears.

The two realized sadly that a squid-like ink of shame and fear must already be clouding the pool of pleasure in the youth's loins. Despair imposed its faint moan and shiver onto the final gasp of orgasm. Their hearts raced. They were sure that the boy's entrails would twist like so much rope when he realized that he was cornered, with no chance of escape. They knew he was imagining himself, his trench coat torn off, dragged naked to the police like a masturbating chimpanzee, with his eyes no bigger than wrinkles and his sodden penis dripping. The jelly of his semen, the color of tears, had already congealed, stiffening his crotch, as he stood before those countless hostile eyes.

J

"A real desperado," J said passionately. "Aren't we going to help him?"

"Yes, let's rescue him if we can," the old man answered. Side by side they approached the man who had caught the youth. They were pale with excitement, as if they were the ones being rescued.

"We'll give him to the police, the rotten *chikan*," the old man said to the indignant man who was holding him. The old man's cheeks were stiff with tension, but he finally managed a slight smile and tried to soften his glittering eyes, which were glazed like a hawk's. The captor looked like a firefighter, but J's friend's imposing physique didn't compare unfavorably. Gently but firmly, the older man overcame the young one. The old man's physical bearing had always fascinated J, and he felt vaguely jealous of the masses of muscle he must have had in his thirties. But J—and J only—could also see that the blades of dissatisfaction were solidly planted in this wild old bull and constantly shivering like the tentacles of bog moss.

"A pervert like this deserves a good beating, doing that to an innocent girl!" The self-righteous citizen had begun to overact.

The wrinkled skin around the old man's eyes was the color of dead leaves, but in an instant of fierce anger, he blushed. The other, mistaking the old man's anger for sympathy with his own indignation, gave him a good-natured nod. J noted how the old man's face, red with anger, resembled the dog on the Gordon's Gin label—it was a resemblance he had noticed the day he first met the old man.

J intervened before the old man got out of hand. "We'll hand him over to the police. If you'll give me your card, we'll let the chief know that it was really you who caught him."

"It is a pleasure to meet people like you who believe in justice. If I had the time, I'd go to the police with you. The damned *chikan*!" the middle-aged man said. He took a creased old business card from the wallet in his inside pocket and handed it to J.

The old man and J held their captive from both sides. They felt his trembling against their sides and hips. "Don't cry, and don't be so stupid as to scream or beg," J whispered in a voice which sounded only in the back of his throat, as the boy shook silently with his eyes downcast. His opponent was comforting the sobbing girl whose orange coat was stained. When he tired to wipe the semen off with his mouse-gray handkerchief, the girl started to scream again. She was pale and seemed about to vomit up bile. The passengers who'd gathered around them laughed in happy and excited voices. For J, seeing this hurt, ugly girl was the only thing that made him feel slightly repelled by the boy who was the cause of this. Why had he rubbed his penis against a girl who was so repulsive and self-righteous and, at the same time, so miserably frightened?

"Listen, miss, this sort of thing won't get you pregnant and you haven't lost your virginity. You are still pure," the man whispered to the girl. His efforts to win himself further glory made the other passengers laugh again. Only now did

J

J and the old man realize that the girl's benefactor smelled of alcohol.

At the next station, the old man and J took the boy's arms and stepped down onto the platform. When the door closed, the departing man waved and smiled, baring his teeth like a monkey. They looked like yellow grains of Indian corn. J tore up the man's business card and threw it away. Then, he turned to the train and, deadly serious, pulled down his lower eyelid to show him the red eye of contempt. Without waiting to see the man's reaction, J and the old man took the boy's arms again (they looked, now, like a happy tri-generational family). As they followed the platform to the stairs, J and the old man took turns giving him advice.

"Your methods are a total mess. It'd be a wonder if you didn't get caught. Why aren't you a little more careful?"

"Besides, you're looking for trouble if you don't do it when there are more people on the train. If you want that kind of excitement, you have to do it when the train is packed."

The old man and J dropped the boy's arms, stopped, and let him go on walking. The rescue had succeeded. Even though he was free, the young man took two or three more steps in the same posture, as if still restrained. Then he paused abruptly and turned around, looking at the old man and J suspiciously. His small nose was no longer bulging, and his eyes were no longer those of a sick dog. The physical serenity that comes after orgasm had given an angelic look to his large face. He looked like a dying martyr after an ordeal, a saint whose sufferings had ended.

"You guys are letting me . . . ?" he asked in a shrill voice. He was unsure, ready to run at any moment.

"No, we're not going to turn you over to the police. That was just a stupid joke," J stammered, as if admitting something difficult. The boy was so serious that his rescuers almost felt ashamed of themselves.

"Today I'd made up my mind to get caught. I wanted to suffer. I meant it, and I went to the point of no return," he said. It was a kind of challenge.

J and the old man looked at each other amazed. When J saw his friend finally manage a smile, he reluctantly smiled himself. It was the smile of a magnanimous boxer who appreciates the strength of his opponent after being fooled by a quick punch to his weak spot. Both were now curious and they gave the boy a more careful look. There was something irritated and resentful about him, but also something sad. The post-orgasmic calm, which had given him the appearance of a gentle saint a few moments before, had disappeared, and the dark shadow of an extremely sharp discontent had replaced it.

"I'm not wearing anything but this coat and these boots. I really suffered before I finally made up my mind to go out like this. And making that final leap into pleasure, with everyone watching me, was as frightening an adventure as closing my eyes and letting go of the handlebars when I'm on a bike doing eighty. I'm like a member of a suicide squad, and you guys turn me into a game?"

J

Tears filled his bloodshot eyes. Suddenly he threw a punch at J, who ruthlessly blocked his forearm, using the boxing techniques he'd learned in college. Groaning in pain, the boy dropped his arms limply and cried a little.

"If you like, we can still hand you over to the subway guards or the police," J threatened. Panting, he glared at the boy and rubbed his wrists, which were starting to turn red.

"That won't be necessary," the boy said. His bleary eyes openly showed signs again of the fear from which he had momentarily recovered.

J saw that the boy was very agitated and emotionally unbalanced, as if he had taken sleeping pills and had yet to fall asleep. This could have been due to some new drug that J didn't know about, but it reminded him of the terribly appealing white tablets of a German sleeping drug to which he had become hopelessly addicted several years earlier. It was the drug J's first wife had used to kill herself. After her death that night, J had tried in vain to redeem himself, but he finally fell into the depths of the fearful unconscious . . .

J's memories took over and dissipated his anger at the boy trying to hit him. Finally, J was smiling.

"Instead of going to the police, why not come to our usual drinking place?" J said with a smile. "It's a bar in a hotel in Unebi-machi."

"I'll go as long as you guys aren't queer. I am not some cute little chick that does fairies, you know," the boy said with a sneer.

J didn't answer. He hadn't slept with a lover of the same

sex for a long time. But still there were times when the sudden craving for a young man's naked body and penis came upon him. But, he thought in self-punishment, I definitely will not have that kind of exciting sexual relationship again. J absolutely wasn't the type to think that a homosexual essence exists inherently in a man as a result of his birth and determines that man to be a life-long homosexual.

"We're not queers, and you can stop calling us 'you guys,'" the old man said.

The old man, J, and the boy had emerged above ground into the dusk of winter. A bit of snow, carried by an intermittent wind, blew against them with persistent repetition. The boy shivered, and several times he hiccuped. First, the old man and J took the boy to a clothing store and bought him some underwear. They had to convince him to go into the toilet to put it on. The boy's lips were swollen blue-black from too much cold and looked like mulberries, and he fell asleep snoring as soon as they got into a taxi. J realized that, after all, he was under the influence of a sleeping drug. The boy slept all the way as the taxi sped through the dangerous snowing evening streets toward Unebi-machi. Occasionally he let out a small yawn and said something in his sleep in a tiny voice. J couldn't get the meaning of his words, but the old man finally understood.

"He seems to have met a monster in his dream, 'I'm afraid, I'm afraid,' he's saying."

"Don't you think it'd be a pretty frightening experience, getting on the subway in nothing but a trench coat and

J

boots? The monster in his dream is probably himself, turned into a *chikan*. He's at that age."

"What do you mean, that age?"

"You know, the age when you have the sensation of fear that feels like there's a monster alive inside you, waiting to be born. From when you're eighteen until about twenty-one or -two."

"I can't imagine such a deep gap between your age and this boy's age. I'm sixty..." the old man started to say and then fell silent. Once he had fallen silent, the old man seemed to be at a complete loss, and before long, he appeared to be tightly closed off, as though he was covered from head to foot in medieval armor. It happened more often that the old man fell silent in the middle of a conversation. With age, his teeth had become like pumice, but he wouldn't let the fierce beast of words escape once he'd bitten into it. When that happened, he would purse his lips and remain silent, casting his hawk-like eyes around him. Whenever J saw an old person like him, he would fantasize about what kind of life they'd lived through. J and the old man were 'street friends.' J didn't know anything about the old man's past or his present position in society. Since they had formed an anti-social relationship, J for his part had never told the old man what kind of person he was either. But J didn't think that he could tell even himself what kind of person he was at the moment. J assumed that the old man was someone who had gone abroad as a diplomat, or had worked as a politician. He guessed as much because they would sometimes meet beside the Ministry of Foreign Affairs or the Diet, and when they did, the old man would be escorted respectfully by a government official or Dietman, looking like he'd just left really spirited dialogue. Nowadays the old man had none of the fishy smell of somebody who's involved in politics. But that day when he'd spotted J standing and waiting at the stairs leading to the subway at the Diet station, he'd waved his hand toward J with an all-too obvious feeling of release in his face. J had felt as though he was being greeted by an ugly old woman. I'm sixty.... J thought about the second half of the man's unfinished sentence. It probably had something to do with old age and death. The old man sometimes talked to J about the fear of death that threatened him, vividly, specifically in the form of cancer or cardiac infarction. I'm sixty, and I know the fearful feeling that the monster called death is rapidly growing inside me: was that what the old man wanted to say? It was as if the old man was giving himself arteriosclerosis of the heart, or he'd secretly stashed a cancer somewhere inside himself, for which an operation would be meaningless, exactly as though he was leaving a precious wine to sleep in a wine cellar. But the old man kept his silence, and didn't speak directly about it....

"Is this boy really a *chikan*? Is he maybe somebody who can't help but be a pervert?" J said to the old man with a smile.

"He seems convinced that he is. And the way he operated today was unique. If you talk about perverts the way a sumo commentator would, you'd say that he has a truly idiosyncratic technique."

"Yes, it sure was unique. That style of attacking while cutting off his path of retreat, it smacked of the overly courageous soldier who has a dangerous suicidal tendency. Still, he's such a child. He must be all of eighteen. Do you think it's possible that he's discovered he can only be a pervert? Or is he one who can't be satisfied with masturbation when he can't find a girlfriend, or who's hysterically afraid of syphilis, or who simply doesn't have the money to buy a whore? In other words, a case of frustrated desire?"

"No, he's probably more of a conscious pervert," the old man said, carefully studying the boy's sleeping face. J felt that like his own, the old man's feelings of goodwill toward the boy were growing deeper. Up until that time, J had continued to be shocked by the violence of the old man's concrete disgust with human beings. He felt that this was the first time since he had become friends from the sidewalk he'd seen him show this kind of magnanimity toward a stranger. Considering the reason why he felt attracted to the boy, J thought it was perhaps because, as the old man had said, his pervert's method of action today had been truly unique. Certainly the boy was alone, filled with fear, a pathetic pervert....

"What he said on the platform, his protest, I don't think was the inspiration of the moment," the old man said. "In any case, he's an interesting boy."

Dirty snow was piled in heaps like earthworks on both

sides of the entrance to the hotel in Unebi-machi. When the
old man and J shook the boy awake, he shivered with cold
as he saw the dirty snow, and a few tears oozed like gum
from between his eyelids.

"Can you walk?" J asked.

"What do you think I am?" the boy said arrogantly,
knitting his brows and giving J back a look of reproach.

The uniformed bellboy who opened the hotel door for
the three of them dragged his big unsightly overshoes like a
pair of weights. They definitely didn't suit his deep green
jacket, or the gold lace frills, or his light blue pants. He'd
probably been intimidated by the snow. Shivering, they
went straight to the bar behind the front desk on the first
floor. They were all relieved it had heating. The old man and
J arranged a pair of chairs in a fan shape facing the chair
where the boy was sitting, as though they'd naturally be
keeping an eye on him. The boy reacted.

"I'm sleepy, so I'll have a whisky," he said before anyone else could speak. He gave his order to the bellboy, who
was still in his overshoes. Both J and the old man asked for
the same. Each drank in silence. The boy came back to life
almost immediately. The three ordered another round of
straight whisky. Trying to save himself some work, the bellboy brought the bottle itself to the table.

"What do you want to ask me? Or do you want me to
say I'm sorry?" the boy said. His defiant attitude hadn't
changed. "Do you have some nasty trick in mind for me?"

"Of course, we'd like to ask you how you got to be a

J

chikan at such a young age. Was it because you wanted to know how hard a girl's ass is? If that's it, you could've just given your own a feel," J said, taking up the boy's challenge.

"You're asking for it, aren't you?" the boy said in a hoarse voice. His whole body began to swell with rage like a mongoose that's come upon a cobra.

"Don't get excited. We want to ask you why you became a *chikan*, and what do you think about being one. We've never seen one as young as you," J said.

"I'm a poet," the boy said proudly.

"A poet?"

"For a long time I've been planning to write a great poem called 'Solemn Tightrope-Walking,'" the boy said with passion. "It's a poem like a tempest, with perversion as its theme. So there's a chicken-and-egg relationship between the poem and me as a pervert. I've been a pervert since I was kid, so I hoped to write a poem about perversion. And to make it an even greater poem, I'm trying to be the most courageous, desperate pervert of them all."

J thought of another young poet he had known. That young poet had once been the lover of J's second wife. While his wife was making her first short film, the lover had been constantly, tenaciously, observing J and his wife in J's apartment and vacation house and in his Jaguar. He had resentful eyes that lurked in the depths of a fog of incombustible desire. In the end, it seemed, the young poet didn't resume his sexual relationship with J's wife. That pacifist with his starved cat's eyes had unexpectedly disappeared from J's world, but what would he be doing now? Had he gone on writing his enervated self-enclosed poetry, trying to pay off the cancer of his unsatisfied desire for J's wife on the installment plan? Whatever the answer, J thought that this boy probably had a richer talent as a poet. As a person, at least, the boy made a more disturbing impression than the docile, plaintive young poet. Here was a man who, with only a trench coat and boots to protect his nakedness, had ejaculated into a crowd of strangers on the subway!

"What's it like then, this poem of yours? Have you written a few lines?" the old man asked enthusiastically, his curiosity aroused.

"Written a few lines? Poetry isn't like that. At least mine isn't. One day I'll know that I've finished the necessary preparation to write this poem. Then I'll start writing, one word per second. It'll take an incredible amount of time, but I won't stop until it's finished," the boy said haughtily.

"But you must have some kind of notes, even if they're only notes in your memory?" J said.

"Oh, those I have, and I've suffered a lot for them. After all, I want to write poetry from experience."

The boy talked about the concept of his poem endlessly. His eloquence increased as he became more and more intoxicated. *Chikans*, you can count tens of thousands of them in Tokyo alone, but they're all solitary, spiritually impoverished matadors of everyday life, filled with a fruitless, dangerous passion, that most solemn of tightrope walkers....

With a look on their faces so stern it's almost beseeching, earnest to the point of ridiculousness, they bare their positions and reputations, at times even their lives to imminent danger. Empty-handed, they act for the merest scrap of trivial passing pleasure. After all, this isn't exactly a golden age for adventurers, is it? Except for those who have the amazing courage to climb into a space ship and then leave the machines to do whatever they want. For two thousand years mankind has joined forces to rebuild this world into a fully rubber-lined nursery, with all danger nipped in the bud! But *chikans* can change this safe nursery into a jungle of savage beasts. As if in a religious ritual, with one action the *chikan*, by putting his fingers on a little girl's thigh for just an instant, puts everything he's built up in life so far in jeopardy.

Chikans have a terribly profound fear of being discovered and punished, but at the same time, without that feeling of danger, their pleasure is diluted, it becomes vague and attenuated, and in the end it's nothing at all. The taboo guarantees the pleasure of the adventure to the tightrope-walkers. But when the *chikans* safely pass their test, in that instant the safe ending destroys the revolutionary meaning the curriculum had when it was still going forward with its results unknown. Eventually the *chikans* realize that, since there wasn't really any danger, the feeling of danger that was the true creature of their pleasure up to that point is nothing but a fake. So the pleasure itself, which they only just finished tasting, is a false pleasure. Thus they have to start their barren tightrope-walking all over again, and continue until they're caught and their lives are in danger. Then, all the dry runs they've undergone up to then make the flower of ecstasy bloom.

Chikans usually perform in silence. When they do talk, both their actions and their words amount to nothing but a lot of laughable running around in circles. The *chikan* is silent, just like a tightrope walker in the circus. But once he's caught, and the hostile eyes of strangers give him his ID badge as a pervert and his true identity as a pervert is confirmed, he can sometimes launch into a kind of self-advertisement that can be moving. During one of the most violent political upheavals in Japan after the war, one *chikan* was caught in the middle of a demonstration of a hundred thousand people who'd surrounded the Diet. When he confessed to the police, he said, "Right now a hundred thousand angry political activists are renouncing their sexual arousal. Now is not the time for that, they say. I was going for the ass of a girl, a nobody in that crowd, and the sexual arousal of all one hundred thousand people was apparently concentrated on my privileged fingers and nothing else. My fingers ignited into a fire of ecstatic, supreme bliss. And, even better, it happened in front of that gigantic police force of the armed Fourth Riot Squad!" It is they who are the serious tightrope walkers of everyday life....

"Not bad," the old man said, "You should write your poem. If you need money to publish it, I'll help you out." J had been about to say the same thing. A boy who was willing to get on the subway on this winter evening with nothing but a trench coat to protect his naked body and face that danger for the sake of a poem, that tempest that he wanted to describe, a terribly anguished boy who, with that desperate look on his face, had soiled the back of an ugly girl's fluffy coat by ejaculating on it, wasn't he what you'd have to call a unique boy, a unique being?

"But the poem forming in my head so far isn't anything like a tempest," the boy said unhappily. "It's what you'd call observational."

"Isn't 'observational' all right?" J said.

"'Observational' doesn't give a poem the greatness of a tempest," the boy said, deep in thought, as though he were a veteran when it came to poetry.

"Well, didn't you take a pretty deep step into the world of your poem today?" J said. "At least you were more than a third-party observer."

"No, it was no good. I was rescued. So my intense fear and my great courage turned into imitations of themselves because today, I felt like I was anticipating, without any reason, that some lifeboat like you two would appear," the boy said.

"But you didn't feel like you were anticipating us until you saw us there. When that public-spirited bogey-man had you, you looked like you were going to have a heart attack any minute," J consoled the boy, half in jest.

"No, I don't think so now. I myself am beginning to feel that it's not true, now that I've been rescued. So it was all wrong," the boy whispered sadly. He sounded dead tired.

His childish face looked infinitely gloomy.

J and the old man became silent and just stared, with pity, at the boy. Couldn't they turn this boy in some other direction, away from the fall into the endless exitless hole that is itself the definition of perversion? Or, because he was burning with desire to write this stormy poem, obsessed by a perversion, should J and the old man have left him in the arms of that despicable, grandiose moralist tied up by the bonds of his own ambition? If they had, he might even now be shivering with cold and shame in a cell in some police station, and be writing, at a single stretch, at a speed of one word per second, for an endlessly long period of time, his poem about "Solemn Tightrope-Walking," a poem with such violence that it would satisfy him.

"Do you plan to have another try tomorrow at that suicidal adventure with no exit, this time making sure that nobody like us can come to your rescue?" J said.

"Tomorrow? It's totally out of the question. I am tired, and I think it's going to take me a long time and a lot more suffering before I can make up my mind about the next adventure. I feel like an idiot who tried to kill himself but was dragged up from the river bottom and, pooh pooh, he started breathing again. His rescuers don't even bother to think about all the bitter ordeals the idiot experienced before he tried to kill himself. All they do is smile and enjoy the rescue, since they pulled him back into the hell-fires of this world using the fire-rake of humanism."

"But why are you so stubborn about getting arrested?

J

Aren't you overestimating the importance of that? Even if you do escape safely, surely that doesn't do anything to harm the meaning of your adventure, does it? You still acted like a pervert," the old man said.

"There are probably all kinds of perverts. I am a poet, so I looked at the sample box and adopted the action methods of the most dangerous type," the boy said, easily evading the old man.

The old man and J looked admiringly at the boy. He certainly gave the impression of being an unfortunate zealot, stuffed full with dangerous and incendiary tension. That was appealing. He seemed to have just passed through the long years of ugliness after escaping the period of infancy. Now he would become more and more beautiful and attractive. But even more than his beauty, the malicious arrogance of the boy had that brilliance particular to his age, and that captured J and the old man.

"When that moralist attacked you, I wanted to give you a shot of camphor so you wouldn't drop dead of a heart attack. For a brave man who chose the most dangerous way to be a pervert, you were pretty scared, weren't you?" J said to the boy after a while.

"Was I really that scared? Then maybe I am gradually approaching the true pervert. Not the conscious pervert whom I've invented in my mind and designed from head to toe, but the pervert who's the true living other, who's more than what's in my head. I'm getting closer to the pervert who's the unexpected other inside me," the boy said. He was concentrating too much passion on his own words to hear J's mockery. J liked this kind of narcissistic person, so he was able to continue his good-natured derision without losing his smile.

"When I was your age I had the same desire to become the other inside me," J said. "To put it simply, it's the child's ardent desire to be an adult." Now he was treating the boy like he was really a child. "We wanted to rescue you, just like any adult who sees a child standing on tiptoe and about to fall over would reach out to support it. In the world of adults, no matter how close you come to the pervert inside your head, you'll always be saved by the adults around you, and you'll be right back where you started. You're Sisyphus Junior, the Pervert, you poor little thing!"

"Maybe that's true, but even so, before that next time, I have to plan my own deadly fatal pattern of perversion, one that's impossible to cancel out, one with which the adults can't interfere. One where instead of keeping me from falling over, the adults of this world will band together to turn me upside down and trample me into the ground," the boy said. He sounded genuinely pathetic, as he again palely shaded the depths of his sleepy, infantile eyes with his dark, miserable weariness. He seemed forlorn, and more like a backward student who doesn't know what to do after failing his exams than a man who would write a violent poem resembling a tempest.

J regretted that he'd carried his ridicule of the boy too far. Feeling embarrassed with himself, he looked at the old man. The old man stared back at him with an air of discomfort. J could imagine what the old man must be thinking: Compared with the straightforward self-confession of this boy, wasn't their own self-defensiveness disgusting? Weren't they protecting themselves like a pair of psychoanalysts in front of a patient? J nodded back at the old man, suggesting, well, aren't we going to tell this boy about ourselves?

"We are perverts who've chosen our sample from the safe side. Of course, being a pervert means there's no such thing as perfect safety, but the two of us follow a policy of joint defense," the old man said.

"What, this bar is a *chikan* club?" the boy shouted out, like he found it all too funny. "Now I see why you saved me, and why you're showing so much interest in me. But why have you formed a *chikan* club instead of being independent perverts?"

"Because it's exactly the perverts who ought to make a club of their own, assuming you want to call it a club," the old man said. "You might take a look at homosexuals. They're oppressed now, like a distinctive group of new blacks. But all around the world they're forming small groups to fight back. Maybe they're thinking they'll make a country for their own kind in the twenty-first century and declare their independence. At the very least, they'll probably elect themselves a few representatives in every country. For people like me, death is only a matter of time and I can only imagine it. But you'll live to see the twenty-first century. You'll see precisely that happen. No doubt they'll produce representatives who are excellent and powerful. But in case you've forgotten, perverts are even more anti-social than homosexuals. The day when homosexuality is no longer a crime probably isn't very far away, but perverts can't expect to see a time when they're exempt from criminality. That's exactly because there are types like you who make arrest and punishment a basic condition of being a pervert. But shouldn't perverts also work out some system of self-defense? That's why we've created this little mutual-aid society. Like we saved you today, we also help each other when one of us is in a tight spot."

This time it was the boy who looked at J and the old man intently. He seemed deeply interested. His expression showed a kind of respect (an attitude of recognizing some individuality in the existence of his counterparts) which had been completely lacking in his speech and actions so far.

"Are you finding a lot of new members for this *chikan* club of yours?" he asked.

"No, there are still just the two of us. But even that's an invention, and a great stride forward in this age of completely solitary perverts. So far this young man and I have been able to avoid arrest," the old man replied with a smile. "How about it, don't you want to join?"

"I don't want anybody to save me, but I could join as a special member and play life-guard to the two of you. Anyway, I haven't decided my next plan of action, and I'm bored. Besides, I'd like to watch some other perverts. The hero of my powerful poem is a dangerous *chikan* like myself, of course, but it might be effective to complicate the structure by casting some more cautious, everyday perverts in supporting roles."

"Well, next time you go out, drop by this bar and meet us, and let's go for a ride on a subway or a train or bus. But until you come up with a new plan for self-destruction, you'll only play the role of rescuing us. After all, that's all you want," J said.

"Yes, that's what I want," the boy said happily. His eyes were no longer shaded with blue-black clouds. Rather, they were just at the point of flaming up with curiosity. The boy put his whisky glass back on the table and sank deep into the sofa. He gave a big yawn and rubbed his eyes hard with his fists, acting as though he'd been blinded. "I'm relieved," he said. "I've gotten sleepy, really sleepy. I thought you might be queers, so I was careful not to go to sleep, but if you're only interested in me as a fellow pervert, I know I don't have anything to worry about. But how did you two happen to organize a *chikan* club? In the very beginning, how did you talk about it? Or are you parent and child by any chance? Don't tell me you're father and son!"

"No, we're not father and son, and we're not brothers either," the old man laughed.

"So first one of you introduced himself as a pervert and said let's start a *chikan* club? That must've taken plenty of courage," the boy said, making a sensitive guess. Psychologically he was now very close to meeting J and the old man halfway. Showing such unguarded curiosity, the boy gave an impres-

Kenzaburo Oe

sion of childishness that was difficult to believe.

"Yes, it took courage. Especially because perverts are not like homosexuals. They don't have something special about them, like a scent you can sniff out. But like today, when we met you, you could say it was the hand of fate that brought us together. If not for that, we never would've even spoken to each other." The old man's voice was happy, and he smiled as he looked at J.

~

One morning, J had decided to become a *chikan*. He had felt very far from the sexual world and had wanted an anti-sexual form of self-punishment, as it were. At the same time, he was driven by a certain sexual excitement, a violent hunger. But at the time of that first conversion he wasn't really aware of the two-headed sex monster that lived inside him. One early winter morning at nine, still in bed after a sleepless night, he had simply thought to himself, *I want to be a* chikan. He'd walked from the bedroom into the main room that his wife used as a work space. She was discussing the script of her new film with her partner, the cameraman.

"You can use the Jaguar if you like," he said. "I'm going to take the train."

"Where are you going?" his wife and the cameraman asked. He said it didn't matter as long as he went by train. So began J's daily routine of roaming the city. Early each morning he left the apartment. Late at night he returned.

J

Usually he found his wife sleeping on the couch in the work space, exhausted, with a blanket drawn up to her chest. Sometimes they barely spoke for days at a time.

Now his wife and the cameraman were planning a completely new film. She had finally succeeded in finishing her first film, but only those who'd taken part in the production had seen it at a few trial screenings. Then the film was bought by a film company for two million yen and burned. At first J's wife had been violently opposed to the idea, but eventually she had no choice but to accept it. This time she wanted to make a film that would show nothing but landscapes and trees. It would be a color film, made with the two million yen as funding. The reason things had turned out the way they had was because of the twenty-year-old actor whom everybody called Boy. He was the cause of all the confusion and bad luck. After the shooting of that first film was finished, while J's wife was persevering in the meandering, time-consuming process of editing the film with her own two hands, the actor appeared in a serial television drama and suddenly became a glittering star. J's wife finished editing her first short film about the same time he was hired by a studio and given his first leading role in a commercial film. The young actor began to dread the scandal that was sure to follow the release of a film that showed him completely naked, living his day-to-day life in hell. He confessed his fear to the producer, and it was conveyed to the chief executives of the studio. That was the start of a difficult dispute, but finally J's wife had yielded. Since the young actor had become a star, J had seen him only once, in a television interview. He hadn't been the same unstable, sharp-witted, freely sexual twenty-year-old youth who was simply floating on the tide. He gave the impression now of firmly planted stability, of being a stolid conformist who only believes in sex within the petty limitations of bourgeois morality. J thought about how he had once wanted to sleep with the actor, but now he felt that it was impossible for him even to think back on the passion he must have had. He wrote this version of "A Star Is Born" in a long letter to his sister, the sculptor, who had returned to Paris. It was a funny, pleasant letter, which apparently had delighted his sister. The film starring the young actor was well received but, according to the cameraman, his beauty in J's wife's film was still beyond comparison. The boy was better in "our film," he said. The young actor no longer appeared at J's apartment.

The exhibitionist jazz singer had also drifted away from the apartment. Rather than becoming a conformist, she was living freely as an increasingly rebellious individual. She'd quit working as a nightclub singer after her involvement in a call-girl ring became the subject of an exposé. Then she began a new life, traveling around Japan with political negotiators visiting from Southeast Asia or staying in hotels with American buyers. The jazz singer was now a high-class prostitute. Occasionally J still received a call from her, but she didn't come to his apartment either. After all, the new film didn't need an actress, and they'd stopped having parties.

J

While J spent his days roaming the city, his wife and the
middle-aged cameraman were alone creating the screenplay
for the new film. They'd locked themselves up in J's apartment for this solitary, gloomy business. Even J didn't go into
the room when they were at work. True enough, J's high-
spirited, pleasurable salon of that morning at the vacation
house looking out over Miminashi Bay had fallen to pieces.
J's wife and the cameraman had developed an even firmer
bond, but all the others had ended up alone and lonely. They
had each begun to live according to their personal choice. In
spite of being a pair, his wife and his old friend the cameraman gave J the same extremely lonely, self-enclosed impression as the others. Even though the two of them were making plans for the new film with almost too much enthusiasm,
they didn't seem to find any particular pleasure in the job.
But then J was almost constantly out of the house, so it was
only by accident that he had time to observe them at work.
His Jaguar had been left in the garage for them to use, but
since the film hadn't yet reached the stage of outdoor locations, it was never driven. Its ivory body was covered with
dust and had lost its sparkle.

Why had he chosen to be a *chikan*? J had never really
given it much thought—somewhere in his heart, he was con-
tinually aware that he was not yet truly deviant. On the
other hand, he realized that, when he finally found himself
humiliated in the strong grip of an angry stranger, he would
have no choice but to think it through. And at times, in the
depths of his being, a flash of what it meant to be a *chikan*

would rise flickering to the surface of his consciousness, like a sudden stay of execution.

One evening J was riding the outbound express from the Tokyo Station on the National Railways Chuo Line. Standing immediately in front of him was a woman of about his age. She was at a right angle to him, and their bodies were pressed together, with her chest, stomach, and thighs fitted to his. J caressed the woman. His right hand moved into the space between her buttocks, while his left hand traveled down her belly toward the space between her thighs. His erect penis was touching the outside of her leg. He and the woman were about the same height. His heavy breath stirred the down on her flushed earlobes. At first J trembled with fear and his breathing was irregular. Was the woman not going to cry out? Would she not seize his arms with her two free hands and call for help from the people around them? When his fear was at its peak, J's penis was hardest. Now it was pressed tight against the woman's thigh. He shook with profound fear as he stared straight at her chiseled profile. Her low, unwrinkled forehead, the bridge of her short, upturned nose, the large lips below a layer of coffee-colored down, the firm jaw, the splendid, dark eyes, cloudy and almost black. She barely blinked at all. As J caressed her rough woolen skirt, he suddenly seemed to lose consciousness. If the girl cried out in disgust or fear, he would have an orgasm. He held on to this fantasy like fear, like desire. But she didn't cry out. She kept her lips firmly closed. Suddenly her eyes closed tightly, like a curtain with its ropes cut falling

J

to the stage. At that instant the restraining pressure of her buttocks and thighs relaxed. Descending, J's right hand reached the depths of her now-soft cheeks. His left hand went to the hollow between her outspread thighs.

J lost his fear and, at the same time, his desire weakened. Already his penis was beginning to wilt. He persisted with his caresses out of curiosity and a sense of duty. He became cool-headed. *This is what always happens*, he thought. *When you can get away with anything, you can never get to that one reality that transcends this condition.* It was nothing more than a step in the same process that had repeated itself time and again since the day he had decided to become a *chikan*, a deviant. Then, suddenly, his fingertips felt the solitary orgasm of this stranger.

A moment later, the train rumbled into Shinjuku Station. J saw the big glistening tears that slipped out from between the woman's tightly shut eyelids rise steadily, break, and run down her cheeks. Her lips were pursed as if she'd bitten into a green plum, carving deep wrinkles that could have been cracks all around her mouth. But at that moment the doors opened and J was pushed out of the car by the human wave, away from the woman and onto the platform. After the train left, he continued to stand on the platform. *She didn't look at me for even a second*, he thought, and he felt so terribly lonely that tears came to his eyes, as they had to hers. He thought of his overwhelming loneliness and fear on the night his first wife had taken sleeping pills and killed herself. He and his wife had been sleeping cheek to cheek. The drug had put her into a deep sleep, and she was snoring loudly. But even in her sleep she was still crying and her tears had awakened him. He knew it was a ridiculous idea, but J thought that if he could meet the woman on the train again, he would want to marry and live with her, even if he had to beg her. For several weeks, at the same time of day, toward evening, he watched out for her at Tokyo Station. But he'd already lost any distinct memory of her looks. It was only the shape and the color and the glistening and falling of her tears that he remembered clearly.

His single encounter with that woman was J's happiest memory as a *chikan*. His dark, unhappy memories were countless. In the early days, all he did, in the trains and the buses, in the department store elevators, was stand petrified and immobilized, pale and dripping with sweat, as he burned with the desire for action. From the time he left his apartment in early morning until late at night, he roamed ceaselessly, like the Flying Dutchman, from one end of Tokyo to the other, but he was unable to actually touch the body of a stranger. That period lasted for several weeks. The day that J became an antisocial activist—in the form of a *chikan*, a molester—he also became extraordinarily sensitive to the presence of society. He discovered all of its various taboos, traps, and hostile restraints; never in his life had he felt this larger society rise up against him with such clamorous self-assertion. People who saw him on the street during that period no doubt believed that he was a man of incompa-

J

rably firm morals. In those days, J was still in the painful period of apprenticeship . . .

Some of the social icons that aroused fear in J were the advertisements that hang down from the ceilings of the trains. If one of those ads bore the words "Encyclopedia for 80 Million," J would feel like a solitary warlord launching an attack on the eighty million citizens of Japan who loved their encyclopedias. He would begin to shiver with the excitement of battle. At such times, the milk-white grips of the train straps, all swaying in unison, were nooses waiting to choke him. He would break out in a sweat and close his eyes.

Even after he'd survived those dark weeks and learned to act freely as a *chikan*, he wasn't always happy. To be a loner in a crowd of strangers, stealthily touching their sexual parts, then escaping safely: that ideally perverse achievement, he thought, must be impossible to enact perfectly. He dreamt of a hunter entering a forest of wild animals, killing a deer, and then leaving it there. The hunter leaves the forest exhausted, but he has tasted a stoic, manly exaltation. When J did battle in the forest of strangers on a rush-hour train and retreated again, he was hoping for that hunter's exaltation, but he almost always faltered halfway and was left dissatisfied, irritated, and humiliated, or he was filled with a useless hatred and found himself indulging in unbridled excesses . . .

One evening J was standing on a large bus that had started from Shibuya. His right hand held the strap, and his left was pressed from behind against the naked skin of a large woman, between her stockings and corset. He was staring straight at the abundant, heavy hair on her massive head, just inches from his eyes. As he smelled her hair, the tension and excitement made his throat so dry it hurt. To hide the fact that he'd raised the woman's heavy·woolen skirt, he was crouching forward with his knees thrust out in front of him, like somebody riding a horse. In this position, it was difficult for him to hold his left hand on the woman's naked thigh. He felt an irritating pain that numbed his arm from his left shoulder to his fingertips, but he endured the pain without moving. Then the woman suddenly dropped her hips as if to lean over and rested her weight on J's unstable left hand. He lost his balance and his head bumped hard against the woman's shoulder. When he managed to stand back up, his left hand was caught firmly in the woman's powerful hand. He was stunned, and began to spin around, to spiral down into a maelstrom of fear. When the bus came to the next stop, the woman pulled him by the hand through the crowd of passengers and out of the bus. He was pale and covered with sweat. His heart was soiled with his own fear and despair, but at the same time he felt some kind of deeper, preordained harmony. It was then he realized for the first time that a desire for self-punishment was part of his fervid lust for the pleasures of a *chikan*. He didn't try to escape. Rather, he walked where the woman led him, like a boy with his mother, to the most contemptuous, cruel policeman of all. But the woman didn't take J to the police. She took him to a room in a cheap hotel, where the walls and ceiling and floor were layered with cardboard to deaden the sound. He

J

tried his best to put an end to his humiliating sexual service as quickly as possible, but he was impotent to the last. The woman lay down in the ugly light of the fluorescent lamp and closed her eyes as if in anguish. Her naked body was covered with yellow fat and looked like the larva of a wasp. She didn't speak, didn't move. J was naked beside her. He pulled up his knees and dropped his head flaccidly. He was in despair. He felt as though the only thing living and moving in that room was the smell of their two naked bodies. Finally he also closed his eyes, and sat huddled and motionless. Offering no resistance, he waited for those hundred years of hell to pass. The woman didn't move either. She was a fox playing dead. It was as if her body was putrefying even as she lay there.

In a crowd, touching a woman's sex beneath her underwear for even an instant excited him to the point where he was ready to risk his entire existence. But when he and the owner of that sex were skin to skin, all of his sexual instincts worked to refuse her. This he understood from such bitter experiences as this one. He was in a constant state of dissatisfaction, but for several months he hadn't had intercourse, even with his wife. Wistfully seeking the slightest opportunity for sexual contact, he became part of the city's crowd of strangers, roaming from morning until late at night. Until the day he met the old man, he had felt utterly alone, more alone than he had ever felt in his life. If he hadn't chanced to meet him, J probably would have become an explosively dangerous deviant, a true *chikan*, and would already have been arrested. In that sense, he felt blessed by the relationship of mutual assistance that he and the old man had established . . .

J was on the Yamanote Line, planning to make a circuit of Tokyo. It was close to the end of morning and a faint winter sun was shining. Almost all the seats in the car were occupied but nobody was standing. The floor was like the gray-black back of a mouse, and dust was rising from it into the sunlight. The passengers were bored, but not so tired as to be distracted. It was a bad moment for a *chikan*.

The situation changed when the train pulled into Ueno Station. A group of about twenty laughing high school girls entered J's car. Their teacher had probably just taken them to see the mummies or the Jomon pottery at the museum. J promptly rose from his seat and made his way into the throng of girls, searching for the most advantageous position for a *chikan*, but before he could get there, he saw a tall old man get up from his seat. The man moved with real agility, but behaved as though nothing unusual was happening. J had a premonition and, his heart pounding, he became an onlooker. The old man was well-built and imposing. In his luxurious camel overcoat, his large chest and broad shoulders towered over the swarm of disagreeable schoolgirls' heads. He had a white silk scarf tied around his thick neck, and a soft hat pulled down over his head. Except for the skin on his face, which was covered with wrinkles the color of dead leaves, and his eyes, which were keen like those of a bird of prey, he was the ideal

J

image of old age, the man you see clutching a golf club in ads for health tonics. Looking at him made you feel better. It let you nurse illusions about your own old age. The high school girls saw several empty seats, but didn't move to sit down. They stood talking with their bodies pressed tightly together, like a herd of zebras threatened by a lion or a flock of scared chickens. Their voices rose above the noise of the train and filled the entire car.

The man's head and upper body didn't show the slightest movement. He slowly let his eyelids droop and, like a child fighting against drowsiness who finally gives in, he closed his eyes. J saw how his skin, and the wrinkles the color of dead leaves around his closed eyelids, gradually turned the color of roses. Now he resembled the drunken, vacuous wild dog on the Gordon's Gin label. Suddenly J realized that the entire group of high school girls had stopped talking. Only the noise of the train could still be heard. The schoolgirls' expressions were ugly and afraid. They were young maidens now, with rough underdeveloped faces, frozen by fear. Only the man with his eyes closed looked happy as he stood there, enraptured, with that rosy glow. J was stricken with fear, as if he himself were in danger. One more minute, and the girls would begin to cry and scream. The stranger would be arrested for indecency.

Just then the train stopped in Nippori, and the doors opened. J jumped up and pushed his way through the schoolgirls until he was in front of the *chikan*. He seized the arm of his camel overcoat, and dragged him by force out onto the platform. The doors closed behind them as soon as they were out of the train. J looked back at the schoolgirls who were glaring at him and the old man from the other side of the glass. The smallest girl in the group, J could see, was blushing crimson red and seemed ready to burst into tears. Probably the old man had touched her breasts or something as he surrendered to his solitary sexual rapture . . .

"You were a little too careless," J apologized as he released his arms from the old man's chest. By this time, he was becoming upset and even felt some self-disgust.

"Thank you. If you hadn't been so kind as to help me, I'm afraid I might've gone all the way," the old man said frankly.

That was how J and the old man became "street friends" and went on to the bar in Unebi-machi to have a drink together.

~

The young man joined J and the old man, and they began to meet regularly at the bar in Unebi-machi before setting out into the crowds of the city. After graduating from high school, the boy hadn't gone on to college or looked for a job. Instead, he had focused all of his passion on writing a stormy poem on perversion. Neither J nor the old man tried to make the boy talk about himself in more detail than that. There was no need for it. They didn't even know one another's names. But almost every day, from morning until evening,

J

sometimes even through the night, the three of them were together, riding subways, loitering on trains and streetcars, on jolting bus trips from Shinbashi to Shibuya. They were a harmoniously matched group. To each other, they were the most loyal of "street friends."

Everything the boy wore was of the highest quality, from his English trench coat (somewhat out of season in mid-winter) to his suits, shirts, ties, and shoes—all somewhat extravagant for his age. But there were many days when he had only a few coins in his pockets and sometimes the old man and J would slip money into his trench coat. It didn't bother him at all and he never refused. He would spend all the money they gave him the same day, on things like garishly decorated leather ski gloves. If he touched a girl's backside with those gloves, she would suspect nothing. Instead, she would imagine that a miniature military tank was running down her flank, they were such completely impractical, ornate gloves.

J, the old man, and the boy went out into the crowds together but, since the boy had joined them, only the old man acted as a pervert while J and the boy devoted themselves entirely to security duties. The boy had made it clear from the start that his intentions were limited to that role, and J unexpectedly found himself standing next to the boy. The old man carried on as before, acting like a veteran *chikan* and showed no interest in the change in J. His zeal bordered on the fanatical and, like J before him, the boy seemed willing to bow before the superiority of the older monster *chikan*.

As they watched over the old man's activities from another corner of the car, J and the boy sometimes discussed what it meant to be a *chikan*. The boy thought incessantly about his stormy poem in praise of sexual deviance, and whenever the conversation turned to the topic, he would become obsessive and talk at length, regardless of their surroundings. The boy, on principle, could not accept deviants who took precautionary measures against danger. He confessed that he had come to feel an awe for the old man, but he, too, had something of the fanatic about him. It was difficult for him to find anything admirable in safety and he consistently rejected anything that muddied the image of the fearless *chikan*, the hero of his stormy poem.

"You, yourself," the boy would say, "you barely get excited by these deviant acts which don't involve any risk in places where there's no danger at all. Isn't it only because this mutual aid between *chikans* isn't one-hundred-percent safe that you can feel some excitement, no matter how small? Didn't the old man say so himself that night when we first talked in Unebi-machi? There's no such thing as perfect safety. A *chikan* is just like a big-game hunter. Most hunters would be bored in a great savanna where the lions and rhinos come purring up to them meek as kittens. A hunter would become neurotic in a place like that!"

J never lost interest in these discussions with the teenager, probably because they forced him to think about his own decision to become a *chikan*.

"Doesn't the idea of a safe *chikan* bother you?" the boy repeated.

J

"You're right, it does. But if it really is the destiny of the deviant to be caught and to experience the ultimate humiliation and taste the greatest danger, there's no need to hurry it, is there? It's the same as death. We're all going to die sooner or later, so what's the point in rushing it?"

"No, it's a mistake to put it that way. If death were the only thing that revealed the meaning of life, I'd want to die as soon as I could. If running the risk of being arrested is one of the intrinsic characteristics of the deviant, then whoever excludes that element can't be a true deviant. He's a fake. In the end he's nothing at all. He'll get bored and fed up with it. The hero of my poem isn't that kind of contemptible character. But what I don't understand is how the old man can be so completely alone when the two of us are here to protect him. It's almost more than I can stand to watch. He looks like a stark naked-*chikan* in real danger," the boy said, watching the old man, who was lost in his own world in the crowded bus, with his eyes closed. His eyelids had already taken on that rosy coloring.

J confided to the boy that he suspected the old man had a nest of cancer lodged in his strong body or that he was deeply worried about his heart symptoms. After that, the boy became more devoted to the old man. Perhaps he was considering giving the dying *chikan* a supporting role in his poem.

The boy often discussed with J his plans for his next decisive deviant action. These plans frightened J. They were clearly criminal, and once the boy had enacted one of them, there would be no way for J and the old man to help him. His plans went beyond the realm of perversity and into that of brutal, sexual crime.

"Forget it. Even if you think only of yourself, you can't do such things. If you do, you'll be forced out of society before you can write your stormy poem. Why do you have to carry things so far to write your violent poem?"

"If you think about it, it might be something I have to do, not for the poem, but so that I can become my true self," the boy said mysteriously.

J didn't really believe the teenager's daydreams, but he had gradually developed a deep feeling of friendship for the boy, and he wanted to try to free him from his fantasies. Perhaps something else was at work in J's mind: J knew that, as a deviant himself, he risked becoming a dangerously spined sea urchin like the boy and that frightened him. So in removing the boy's spines, he was in fact hoping to protect himself . . .

Late one night, when J and the old man were alone in the hotel bar in Unebi-machi, J made a suggestion.

"I think I'll take the boy to see a girl I've known for a while, a kind of semi-prostitute. It might be better for him if we could shift his poetic interest away from perverted heroes to more lyrical poems about sensual love."

"You should try. If he wants to become a *chikan*, he's still got plenty of time to change—he can do it at sixty," the old man laughed.

So J called his friend the jazz singer and took the boy to

J

her place. She had been living for quite a long time in a hotel in Shinbashi. He explained the situation and persuaded her that the boy should experience a completely normal sexual relationship at least once. The boy smiled vaguely as he listened to J's pleading. He asked J to wait in the hotel bar because he felt a little nervous. The boy's words seemed to flatter the reckless jazz singer. But it was the jazz singer who called J on the phone, practically in tears as she screamed, "Come and get this monster out of here!" J had barely finished his first glass of Pernod. By the time he got to the room, the boy was sitting serenely on a chair, with his tie carefully knotted, smiling the way he always did. The woman was in the shower, making frantic, violent sounds as if out of her mind. J looked into the bathroom to say he was taking the boy with him. When she turned to look at him, she was ghostly pale, perhaps (or perhaps not) because of the icy shower. "I'm finished with you too," she screamed at J. As J closed the door, he noticed some drops of blood on the tiles beside the bathtub. The boy didn't say anything, and J didn't question him. He had done something terrible.

From then on, neither J nor the old man made any special attempt to intervene in the boy's affairs. The three calmly resumed their "street friends" habit of cruising the city, but they knew that, ultimately, the boy was not there to stay. He was merely resting, sheltered by J and the old man, before embarking on his second major deviant act. He was a traveler taking a brief respite.

Kenzaburo Oe

~

Winter was coming to an end. At night, thunder rolled through the sky and intermittent rain poured down. In early morning, the sun spread its warmth, still tepid as a cat's belly. J's wife made a schedule of outdoor locations with the cameraman and pasted it to the wall of the work space. They would probably be shooting her new film from spring through early summer. One morning J met the old man and the two of them went to the bar in Unebi-machi. For several days, the boy had stayed away from them. He seemed to have fallen into a depression. And by now, when the boy wasn't around, both J and the old man felt their excitement at a lower level when they entered the crowd. So, that morning, neither of them could resist a warm smile when they discovered the boy waiting for them at the hotel bar in Unebi-machi. J remembered—though only vaguely—how the old man's face used to fill with such pleasure that it was nearly ugly when he caught sight of J in the days when they were still only two. And just as J had been then, the boy was clearly in a bad mood, as if he disliked both of them. He placed a bottle of sleeping pills and a tumbler of whisky on the low table in front of his chair. They said nothing about the fact that he was mixing liquor and pills so early in the morning, but they couldn't watch his behavior with indifference. They tried to relax and smile as they shifted in their chairs, in silence, facing the boy.

"I've finished my second period of preparation," the

J

boy said. "I'm going to do it."

The old man and J looked at him. Their smiling cheeks and lips stiffened. The boy's face was flushed with warmth by the sleeping pills and whisky. He had a cunning expression that vividly reminded the old man and J of the night they had met him, desperate, wearing only boots and a trench coat over his naked body. His eyes were bloodshot and seemed to bulge, and his face was deadly pale and dirty. His voice quavered hysterically, the hoarse voice of an angry child.

"But you're wearing a suit today. And you even have your pants on, haven't you? Are you going to lock yourself up in a restroom somewhere and change into your light-weight uniform?" the old man said to the boy. His awkwardly derisive tone seemed to be meant to hide his uneasiness.

"No, I won't do the same thing as before. Didn't I tell you so the first time when you got in my way?" the boy said. When he said "got in my way" instead of "rescued me," J felt as if the boy were spitting on his friendship.

"You aren't seriously going to carry out one of the crazy fantasies you told me about—raping someone on the train or stabbing an old woman to death on the subway," J said, trying to stay calm.

"I'm not telling anyone about my plans. The minute I do, they will vanish into thin air like a mirage. Anyway, can't you just leave me alone now? All I promised when I joined you was to be the special lifeguard for this *chikan* club. So from now on, just leave me alone!" the boy said.

"If that's the case, why did you go to so much trouble to tell us you've finished your preparations and you're ready for your second big adventure? Shouldn't you have kept quiet and gone off somewhere to carry it out alone?"

"I only came to say goodbye," the boy said. "After all, aren't we friends?" He was so frank and honest that it moved J and the old man. Then his radiant, bloodshot eyes clouded with tears, and he stood up roughly, like a violent child. "Don't get in my way. It nearly killed me, the pain and suffering it took to make up my mind to go through with it this time. I've made my sacrifices, and I've made up my mind, so I want you to get out of my way. I really can't stand you safe deviants, in it half for the fun. If you try to stop me, I'll go to the police and tell them what a pair of *chikan* you two really are!"

The boy left the hotel at a run. The old man and J paid the bill and followed him. The sidewalk was dry and no longer showed any trace of snow. J and the old man were breathing hard as they tailed the boy, who was taking long strides, as if driven by anger. He was heading toward the National Railways Unebi-machi Station. Suddenly he turned his head slyly. When he saw J and the old man, he made a gesture to show that his annoyance was getting the better of him. He stood motionless and continued to glare at them. J and the old man approached him hesitantly.

"Why are you following me?" the boy shouted. He had lost his equilibrium under the repeated assault of sleeping pills and whisky. He was no longer his normal self. His sturdy upper body was slowly tilting to one side, then suddenly became erect, and then began to lean again.

"It's gone to your head. Go home and sleep. We'll take you there by taxi."

"Why are you following me? Don't you know this is none of your business? This is important to me!" the boy was screaming and waving his arms as if to threaten them. They were in a busy shopping street, and people began to gather immediately.

"Okay, we won't interfere. But you can't stop us from watching your adventure, can you? We want to be there when you become a *chikan* of the dangerous type. I mean, I can't imagine you're going to have the freedom to write your stormy poem after you go through with this adventure. So go on and do what you have to do. Don't worry about us rescuing you or getting in your way. If you're afraid now, I guess it must be real fear you're feeling," J said. He had gradually become more and more irritated, and in the end he'd spoken with hatred.

For just an instant, a meek, surprised expression returned to the boy's face, and he stared at J. Then suddenly he turned and began to walk away. He didn't look back again, and was absorbed in himself, as if he'd already completely forgotten them. They followed him at a distance of about a hundred feet, without speaking.

The boy went into the Unebi-machi Station. After he'd passed through the gate, J and the old man went to the ticket window. They bought their tickets without hurrying, and by the time they passed through the gate, the boy had already begun to work. He was standing next to a vendor's booth sandwiched between two sets of stairs that diverged in a fan shape toward the platforms for Kanda and Ikebukuro. In his right hand, he held the hand of a little girl. With his left hand, he was holding up a toy for her to see. It was a red battery-powered monkey. He leaned forward a little and said something to the girl. Then he gave her the toy monkey and, side by side, the two of them climbed the stairs to the platform on the Kanda-bound side. They gave an impression of shared, secret intimacy, as if they were brother and sister, which made the people who watched them smile. Only J and the old man did not smile. They realized that the boy intended to kidnap the girl, but they were struck dumb by the fear that realization aroused.

When the teenager and the child had reached the top of the stairs and disappeared from sight, the door of the bathroom behind the vendor's booth was pushed open and a young woman came out. She looked around and called out to someone in a low timid voice. Then, as if prompted by fear, she started up the stairs toward the Ikebukuro platform, crying out the child's name. She seemed about to fall several times, but she climbed the stairs with agility. At the same time, the old man and J took one step forward. They wanted to shout to the woman, to warn her to take the other stairs. But they both remained silent. Their lips were tightly closed, and their hands dangled uselessly. Could they be still under the spell of the teenager's words?

J

A second later, the woman's cry of protest descended on them like a plummeting kite. J didn't have time to look back at the old man. He ran up the stairs the boy and the little girl had climbed, taking several steps at a time. He arrived at an excruciating, pathetic scene. A Yamanote Line train was rumbling in along the platform. On the opposite platform, the young woman was stretching out her arms, about to dive onto the tracks. The little girl who was clutching the red monkey was struggling in the ditch of iron-colored gravel between the tracks. The boy was on his knees on the track where the train was approaching. Throwing the girl into the safe ditch, he had twisted the top half of his body upward like a fallen horse. His arms were now empty and he seemed about to neigh at the sky. He folded them tightly against his chest. Just before J closed his eyes, he saw something that was like a strange, wondrous vision: the front of the train was suddenly dyed crimson red with the boy's blood. J screamed and started to cry.

An hour later, J and the old man were sitting shoulder to shoulder on a couch in the hotel bar in Unebi-machi. In silence, each of them stared at the other's trembling glass. J recalled the words of the sobbing young woman as she appealed over and over to the crowd that had gathered around her. "That man was a god," she said, holding the little girl to her chest. "My little girl saw me and jumped from the platform down onto the tracks. Everybody could see she was going to be killed! I could see it too. But that man, like a god he was, he saved her, and then the poor thing . . . "

186

"When's all said and done, that boy was simply trying to live his life as a *chikan*. If I think of that, it gives me a miserable bit of peace of mind," the old man said. "But a *chikan*, even if he risks his life as that boy did, cannot but continue to be a *chikan*. He was a dangerous man. A club of safe deviants like us is, in my opinion, simply a way of diluting the poison."

"The boy said the same thing to me more than once," J said.

"In the end, there's something fraudulent about us. I've realized that we either have to become dangerous deviants who take risks like him, or we have to give it up altogether. Those are the only two possible roads," the old man said.

"I feel the same way. I'll probably never come to this bar after today, and I doubt I'll have the honor of meeting you again," J said with deep sorrow.

"You'll probably stop being a *chikan*. And I'll become a more dangerous one, I suppose. I've had this presentiment that someday I'll be arrested in a crowd on the subway and die of a cardiac infarction."

J stood up. The old man remained seated, looked up at J, and shook his head. He blushed around his eyes and smiled sadly—like the drunken wild dog on the Gordon's Gin label—as he did when he was burning with anger or sexually aroused. A mist of white tears covered his predatory eyes. They were the gentlest eyes the old man had ever shown to J. J was moved to tears again. Like the old man, he smiled slightly, shook his head, and remained silent. He left

J

the bar and the hotel. He was lightheaded and afraid that he might collapse while the old man was watching him. In the taxi the bellboy had found for him, J was utterly desperate and choked with tears. He'd just lost the two best friends he'd ever had.

~

J spent the next couple of weeks holed up in his apartment. During that time, he realized that it was a burden and a source of pain for his wife that he never went out of the house anymore. And not only for his wife. The cameraman, who was coming regularly to the work space to do pre-production work on the film, showed the same reaction to J's presence. But since J was thinking about nothing but the boy and the old man, he didn't pursue the deeper meaning of these reactions. He was as uncomprehending as an infant.

His own feelings were such that even when the cameraman finally came into his bedroom late one morning and solemnly said there was something he wanted to talk about, J still thought it must have to do with the film's production costs or the need to use the Jaguar. But the cameraman confessed that he had fallen in love with J's wife and, as a result, she was pregnant. J stared in disbelief at the middle-aged man with his ridiculous moustache planted on a face that was big and round and black as a whale's, staring at him with bloodshot eyes. It seemed perfectly natural to J that he experienced no particularly cruel feelings of pain. How on earth could this be? How could something like this possibly happen between this passionate outsider, a middle-aged man who loved precision instruments, and J's wife, with her meager, boyish body, who was only interested in making films? J found it hard to believe. And could his wife, with her unfeminine hips, really be capable of pregnancy? She'd probably die during childbirth.

"I know it must be a shock to you to be betrayed by your oldest friend. Isn't it, J?" the cameraman said, as though he was trying to comfort him. Oldest friend? J objected to that. The only beings the word *friend* truly evoked for him now were a dead teenager and a solitary old man who at this very minute was undoubtedly roaming the crowded streets.

"Well, how long has it been going on?" J asked. It was a stupid question, and he blushed at the meaninglessness of his own words. Once he found out how long they'd been betraying him, then what would he do?

But the cameraman gave him an earnest answer. "Ever since you started staying away from home, J."

"And you got her pregnant in the middle of the afternoon?" J said derisively.

The cameraman's large, round, dark face blushed copper red. He stammered and spoke in a trembling voice.

"J, you are sexually perverted. From what Mitsuko has told me, it's clear that you've been using her sexually as a substitute for a boy, as a homosexual partner. To be blunt about it, when a sexually perverted man is married, another man *should* have a sexual relationship with the wife. It's his duty."

J imagined the cameraman and his wife gossiping about his sexual proclivities, and, for the first time, he was seized with a fierce anger. The cameraman seemed to be waiting for a beating, which he intended to endure without resistance. In the end, J didn't resort to violence. Instead he felt the cancer of self-loathing, which had lodged itself so persistently in the recesses of his heart since he'd beaten the cameraman in the mountain house overlooking Miminashi Bay, beginning to dissolve.

"So what do you intend to do?" J asked with affection while he looked into the cameraman's red, insecure eyes, which had become so familiar to him over these last years.

"I'll marry Mitsuko and we'll have the child, assuming you'll give her a divorce," the cameraman said excitedly.

"And what about your own wife and child?"

"I suppose I'll give them an allowance. If I can, I'd like to take care of the child myself, though."

"It's going to be tough," J said.

"Yes, it'll be tough. And we still have to finish the film," the cameraman said. His dull, fixed expression, so middle-aged, was gradually changing, beginning to glow with a proud self-confidence. J felt pity and compassion for him, but he wondered how many people would have to suffer the hardships of the real world for the sake of this man's recklessness, this man who could easily have been a tribal leader in some patriarchal society.

"I'll file the divorce papers as soon as I can," J said. "Have you already looked for somewhere to live with Mitsuko?"

"No, not yet."

"Then I'll leave. I can move in with my father for a while," J said.

"About the movie . . . "

"I'll give you the 16-millimeter Arriflex. Mitsuko has money in the bank in her own name, from selling the first film. And you don't need to worry about the money my father invested."

"J, thank you," the bearded cameraman said. He was moved. Suddenly his shoulders began to shake as softly as a woman's, releasing all the tension from his body. He returned to the work space with childish sobs in the back of his throat.

For some time J stayed in bed, lying on his back without moving. No thoughts came to him. Occasionally he could hear his wife and the cameraman whispering in the work space. Then he packed his clothes and personal belongings in a suitcase, went down the kitchen stairs to the garage without speaking to his wife, and, for the first time in months, got into the Jaguar. J drove to the headquarters of a steel company in Marunouchi to visit his father, who was president of the company. He told his father about the divorce and asked him to understand what had happened and why he would be moving back into his father's house that same day. J's father smiled gently as he heard J out. Then he asked, "How old are you?"

J

"I'm thirty," J replied. The word *thirty* echoed oddly in his ears. In some strange way he felt guilty. Thirty? At this age, he was no longer a child.

"You've lived like a fugitive in hiding ever since your first wife killed herself. But now your second wife has been sleeping with another man, and she's leaving you. Doesn't that even things up? How about it? You're thirty already, aren't you about ready to start leading a normal life again? This company is building a revolutionary mercury-alloy plant, and as part of the groundwork, I'm going on a tour of our American partners. Why don't you come along as my secretary? And why don't you take a job at the new plant? I'll show you some slides of a forty-story building that was built with nothing but this alloy. It'll excite you. It's something worth doing. I know you're going to take me up on my offer and start a new life for yourself!"

J thought about the offer as he sat watching the slide show with his father. Now that his old friends and wife had left him, one new friend had died in an accident, and the other had vanished into the crowd of ten million people in Tokyo, he was completely alone. This was certainly a chance to return to his old conformist life. To his real life. Of course he knew that it was self-deception, even emotionally, to cancel out his sense of responsibility and guilt for his first wife's suicide with his second wife's adultery and betrayal. But wasn't the very act of acknowledging that self-deception the first step in his rehabilitation to the life of a conformist? He felt that he was beginning now to lay one self-deception on top of another and would go on doing so until he was indistinguishable from the aging monster who was sitting beside him, growling like a disgruntled animal as he watched his color slides. It felt like resignation, and at the same time it felt like being rescued after drifting at sea for too long, even if it was rescue by an enemy ship . . .

In the end J gave in to his father and accepted the offer. His departure for America was three weeks away. His daily life would suddenly turn full circle. As he left the president's office, walked down the long corridor, and got into the elevator, he imagined his father, whom he had just left, as the image of himself forty years from now. His father now and himself in forty years, both would remain perfectly composed even if they had cancer or faced the risk of cardiac infarction. Neither would ever lose the poker face of the old conformist monster. Yes, his new life as a self-deceiving conformist had just begun. Swinging his shoulders vigorously like a busy, capable, company man, he exited through the automatic door of the building and headed toward his Jaguar, which was parked next to the subway entrance. Suddenly he was so excited he thought he would faint. Abandoning the Jaguar, he ran, nearly jumped, down the stairs into the subway.

He boarded a crowded subway car and, without hesitating, advanced steadily through the tight throng of bodies. With no uncertainty, almost as if by prior arrangement, he arrived at a spot behind a young woman. He took a quick

J

look around. The sound of hot blood ringing in his ears had already swallowed up the rumbling of the train and the noise of the passengers' voices. He closed his eyes tightly and rubbed his naked penis repeatedly in the warm intimacy of the girl's buttocks. They were fat as a pheasant's and they offered him resistance. At once he saw himself as someone who was taking a step forward with no possibility of retreat. A new life, a new life with no deception. With low moans sounding in his blazing head, he climaxed.

All the outside clamor sprang to life again. Surely and ineradicably staining the woman's coat, his semen was real, a piece of evidence. The ten million strangers of Tokyo glared at J with hostile eyes. *J!* they seemed to call. Fear struggled against bliss in a wave that rose up interminably and engulfed him. Countless arms had seized him. Overcome with fear, J began to cry. He considered his tears to be his compensation for those his wife had cried the night she killed herself.